The
Swallows
of
Kabul

The Swallows of Kabul

The
Swallows
of
Kabul

✶

Yasmina Khadra

TRANSLATED FROM THE FRENCH
BY JOHN CULLEN

WILLIAM HEINEMANN : LONDON

First published in the United Kingdom in 2004 by William Heinemann

1 3 5 7 9 10 8 6 4 2

Copyright © Éditions Julliard, Paris, 2002

English language translation copyright © 2004 by John Cullen

Yasmina Khadra has asserted his right under the Copyright, Designs and Patents Act, 1988 to be identified as the author of this work

The Swallows of Kabul was first published in France in 2002 by Julliard, Paris, under the title *Les Hirondelles de Kaboul*

This edition published by arrangement with Nan A. Talese, an imprint of Doubleday, a division of Random House, Inc

William Heinemann
Random House Group Limited
20 Vauxhall Bridge Road, London, SW1V 2SA

Random House Australia (Pty) Limited
20 Alfred Street, Milsons Point, Sydney,
New South Wales 2061, Australia

Random House New Zealand Limited
18 Poland Road, Glenfield
Auckland 10, New Zealand

Random House (Pty) Limited
Endulini, 5a Jubilee Road, Parktown, 2193, South Africa

Random House UK Limited Reg. No. 954009

www.randomhouse.co.uk

A CIP catalogue record for this book
is available from the British Library

Papers used by Random House
are natural, recyclable products made from wood grown in
sustainable forests. The manufacturing processes conform to
the environmental regulations of the country of origin

ISBN 0 434 01141 X

Printed and bound in Great Britain by
Mackays of Chatham Ltd, Chatham, Kent

IN THE MIDDLE of nowhere, a whirlwind spins like a sorceress flinging out her skirts in a macabre dance; yet not even this hysteria serves to blow the dust off the calcified palm trees thrust against the sky like beseeching arms. Several hours ago, the night, routed by the dawn and fleeing in disorder, left behind a few of its feeble breezes, but the heat has scorched and smothered them. Since midday, not a single raptor has risen to hover above its prey. The shepherds in the hills have disappeared. For miles around, apart from a few sentries crouched inside their rudimentary watchtowers, there is not a living soul. A deathly silence pervades the dereliction as far as the eye can see.

The Afghan countryside is nothing but battlefields, expanses of sand, and cemeteries. Artillery exchanges shatter prayers, wolves howl at the moon every night, and the wind, when it breathes, mingles beggars' laments with the croaking of crows.

Everything appears charred, fossilized, blasted by some unspeakable spell. Erosion grinds away with complete impunity, scratching, rasping, peeling, cobbling the necrotic soil, erecting monuments to its own calm power. Then, without warning, at the foot of mountains singed bare by the breath of raging battles, rises Kabul, or rather, what's left of it: a city in an advanced stage of decomposition.

The cratered roads, the scabrous hills, the white-hot horizon, the pinging cylinder heads all seem to say, *Nothing will ever be the same again.* The ruin of the city walls has spread into people's souls. The dust has stunted their orchards, blinded their eyes, sealed up their hearts. In places, the buzzing of flies and the stench of animal carcasses declare the irreversibility of the general desolation. It seems that the whole world is beginning to decay, and that its putrefaction has chosen to spread outward from *here*, from the land of the Pashtuns, where desertification proceeds at a steady, implacable crawl even in the consciences and intellects of men.

Nobody believes in miraculous rains or the magical transformations of spring, and even less in the dawning of a bright new tomorrow. Men have gone mad; they have turned their backs on the day in order to face the night. Patron saints have been dismissed from their posts. Prophets are dead, and their ghosts are crucified even in the hearts of children. . . .

And yet it is also here, amid the hush of stony places and the silence of graves, in this land of dry earth and arid hearts, that our story is born, like the water lily that blooms in a stagnant swamp.

One

ATIQ SHAUKAT flails about him with his whip, trying to force a passage through the ragged crowd
swirling around the stalls in the market like a swarm
of dead leaves. He's late, but he finds it impossible to
proceed any faster. It's like being inside a beehive; the
vicious blows he deals out are addressed to no one in
particular. On souk day, people act as if in a trance.
The throng makes Atiq's head spin. In thicker and
thicker waves, beggars arrive from the four corners
of the city and compete with carters and onlookers
for hypothetically free spaces. The porters' effluvia
and the emanations of rotting produce fill the air
with an appalling stench, and a burden of relentless
heat crushes the esplanade. A few spectral women,
segregated inside their grimy burqas, extend imploring hands and clutch at passersby; some receive a
coin for their trouble, others just a curse. Often,
when the women grow too insistent, an infuriated
lashing drives them backward. But their retreat is

brief, and soon they return to the assault, chanting their intolerable supplications. Others, encumbered by brats whose faces are covered with flies and snot, cluster desperately around the fruit vendors, interrupting their singsong litanies only to lunge for the occasional rotten tomato or onion that an alert customer may discover at the bottom of his basket.

"You can't stay there!" a vendor shouts at them, furiously brandishing a long stick above their heads. "You're bringing my stall bad luck, not to mention all kinds of bugs."

Atiq Shaukat looks at his watch and clenches his teeth in anger. The executioner must have arrived a good ten minutes ago, and he, Atiq, is still dawdling in the streets. Exasperated, he starts hitting out again, wielding his many-thonged whip in an effort to part the flood of humanity, futilely harrying a group of old men as insensible to his blows as they are to the sobs of a little girl lost in the crowd. Then, taking advantage of the opening caused by the passage of a truck, Atiq manages to squeeze into a less turbulent side street and hastens, despite his limp, toward a building that stands oddly upright amid an expanse of rubble. Formerly a clinic, but fallen into disuse and long since ransacked by phantoms of the night, the building is used by the Taliban as a temporary prison on the occasions when a public execution is to take place in the district.

"Where have you been?" thunders a large-bellied, bearded man stroking a Kalashnikov. "I sent someone to fetch you an hour ago."

Without slackening his gait, Atiq says, "I beg your pardon, Qassim Abdul Jabbar. I wasn't home." Then, in a resentful voice, he adds, "I was at the hospital. I had to take my wife. It was an emergency."

Qassim Abdul Jabbar grumbles, not at all convinced, and puts a finger on the face of his watch, indicating to Atiq that everyone's growing impatient, and all because of him. Atiq hunches his shoulders and heads toward the building, where armed men waiting for him are squatting on either side of the main door. One of them stands up, dusts off his behind, walks over to a pickup truck parked about sixty feet away, climbs inside, guns the motor, and backs up to the prison entrance.

Atiq Shaukat extracts a ring of keys from under his long vest and rushes into the jail, followed by two militiawomen hidden inside their burqas. In a corner of the cell, in a pool of light directly under a small window, a veiled woman has just finished her prayers. The other two women, the ones from the militia, ask the prison guard to withdraw. Once they are alone, they wait for the prisoner to rise to her feet. Then they approach her, unceremoniously command her to keep still, and begin to bind her tightly, pinioning her arms to her sides and trussing her legs together at midthigh. Having verified that the cords are pulled taut and solidly knotted, they envelop the woman in a large sack of heavy cloth and push her ahead of them into the corridor. Atiq, who is waiting at the door, signals to Qassim Abdul Jabbar that the militiawomen are coming. He, in turn, tells the men in front of the jail to move away. Intrigued by the proceedings, a few onlookers form a silent group at some distance from the building. The two militiawomen step out into the street, seize the prisoner by her armpits, push and haul her up into the back of the truck, load her onto the bench, and sit beside her, so close that she's pinned between them.

Abdul Jabbar raises the truck's side rails and fastens the latches. He takes one last look at the militiawomen and their prisoner to assure himself that all is as it should be, then climbs into the cab beside the driver and strikes the floor with the butt of his weapon to signal the beginning of the procession. The truck pulls away at once, escorted by an enormous 4 × 4 topped with a rotating light and packed with slovenly militia soldiers.

MOHSEN RAMAT hesitates for a long time before he decides to join the crowd gathering in the square. The authorities have announced the public execution of a prostitute: She is to be stoned to death. A few hours earlier, workers came to the execution site to unload wheelbarrows filled with rocks and dig a small hole about two feet deep.

Mohsen has been present at many lynchings of this nature. Just yesterday, two young men—one of them barely a teenager—were hanged from a traveling crane mounted on the back of a truck; their bodies were not taken down until nightfall. Mohsen loathes public executions. They make him conscious of his vulnerability, they sharpen his perception of his limits, they fill him with sudden insight into the futility of all things, of all people. At such times, there's no longer anything to reconcile him to his certitudes of days gone by, when he would raise his eyes to the horizon only to lay claim to it. The first time he watched someone put to death—a murderer, whose throat was slit by a member of his victim's family—the sight made him sick. For many nights thereafter, his sleep was dazzled by nightmarish visions. He started awake more than once, shouting like a man possessed. But time has passed, and scaffolds have come to seem more and more a part of ordinary life, so much so that the citizens of Kabul grow anxious at the thought that an execution might be postponed. Now expiatory victims are dispatched in droves, and Mohsen has gradually stopped dreaming. The light of his conscience has gone out. He drops off the moment he closes his eyes, he sleeps soundly until morning, and when he wakes up, his head is as empty as a jug. For him and everyone else,

death is only a banality. Moreover, everything is banality. Apart from the executions, which are the
mullahs' way of setting their house in order, there's
nothing at all. Kabul has become the antechamber to
the great beyond: a dark antechamber, where the
points of reference are obscure; a puritanical ordeal;
something latent and unbearable, observed in the
strictest privacy.

Mohsen doesn't know where to go or what to do
with his idleness. Every day, starting in the morning,
he roams through the devastated areas of the city
with a vacillating mind and an impassive face. In the
old days—that is, several light-years ago—he loved
to take an evening stroll along the boulevards of
Kabul. Back then, the windows of the bigger stores
didn't have very much to offer, but no one came up
to you and struck you in the face with a whip. People went about their business with enough motivation to envision, in accesses of enthusiasm, fabulous
projects. The smaller shops were filled to bursting; a
hubbub of voices poured out from them and spilled
onto the sidewalks like a flood of friendliness and
goodwill. Settled into wicker chairs, their fans laid
carelessly across their bellies, old men smoked their
water pipes, occasionally squinting at a sunbeam.
And the women, despite wearing long veils and
peering through netting, pirouetted in their perfumes like gusts of warm air. The caravan travelers

of bygone days used to swear that they had nowhere and never, in all their wanderings, encountered such bewitching beauties. They were inscrutable vestals, their laughter a song, their grace a dream of delight. And this is the reason why the wearing of the burqa has become a necessity, more to preserve women from malicious eyes than to spare men the temptations of infinite allurements. . . . How far off those days seem. Could they be nothing but pure fabrications? These days, the boulevards of Kabul are no longer amusing. The skeletal facades that by some miracle are still standing attest to the fact that the cafés, the eating places, the houses, and the buildings have all gone up in smoke. The formerly black-topped streets are now only beaten tracks scraped by clogs and sandals all day long. The shopkeepers have put their smiles in the storeroom. The *chilam* smokers have vanished into thin air. The men of Kabul have taken cover behind shadow puppets, and the women, mummified in shrouds the color of fever or fear, are utterly anonymous.

At the time of the Soviet invasion, Mohsen was ten years old, an age when one fails to understand why, all of a sudden, the gardens are deserted and the days as dangerous as the nights; an age when one is particularly ignorant of how easily great misfortunes happen. His father had been a prosperous merchant. The family lived in a large residence in the very center of the city and regularly entertained relatives and friends. Mohsen doesn't remember much from that period, but he's certain that his happiness was complete, that no one challenged his outbursts of laughter or condemned him for being a spoiled, capricious child. And then came the Russian tidal wave, with its apocalyptic armada and its triumphant massiveness. The Afghan sky, under which the most beautiful idylls on earth were woven, grew suddenly dark with armored predators; its azure limpidity was streaked with powder trails, and the terrified swallows dispersed under a barrage of missiles. War had arrived. In fact, it had just found itself a homeland. . . .

The blast of a horn propels him to one side. Instinctively, he puts his long scarf up to his face as a shield against the dust. Abdul Jabbar's truck grazes him, just misses a muleteer, and hurtles into the square, closely followed by the powerful 4 × 4. At the sight of this cortege, an incongruous roaring shakes the crowd, where shaggy adults and slender youths vie for the choicest places. To calm people down, militiamen distribute a few savage blows.

The vehicle comes to a stop in front of the freshly dug hole. The sinner is helped down while shouts of abuse ring out here and there. Once again, waves of movement perturb the crowd, catapulting the less vigilant into the rear ranks.

Insensible to the violent attacks intended to eject him, Mohsen takes advantage of the agitation, slips through the gaps it opens in the throng, and gains a spot near the front. Standing on tiptoe, he watches a fanatic of colossal proportions lift up the impure woman and "plant" her in the hole. Then, to keep her upright and prevent her from moving, he buries her in earth up to her thighs.

A mullah tosses the tails of his burnoose over his shoulders, addresses a final glare of contempt to the mound of veils under which a person is preparing to die, and thunders, "There are some among us, humans like ourselves, who have chosen to wallow in filth like pigs. In vain have they heard the sacred Message, in vain have they learned what perniciousness lurks in temptation; still they succumb, because their faith is insufficient to help them resist. Wretched creatures, blind and useless, they have shut their ears to the muezzin's call in order to hearken to the ribaldries of Satan. They have elected to suffer the wrath of God rather than abstain from sin. How can we address them, except in sorrow and indignation?"

He stretches out an arm like a sword toward the mummy. "This woman knew exactly what she was doing. The intoxication of lust turned her away from the path of the Lord. Today, the Lord turns His back on her. She has no right to His mercy, no right to the pity of the faithful. She has lived in dishonor; so shall she die."

He stops to clear his throat, then unfolds a sheet of paper amid the deafening silence.

"*Allahu akbar!*" yells someone in the back of the crowd.

The mullah raises an imperious hand to silence the shouter. After reciting a verse from the Qur'an, he reads something that sounds like a judgment, returns the sheet of paper to an interior pocket of his vest, and at the end of a brief meditation proposes that his listeners arm themselves with stones. This is the signal. In an indescribable frenzy, the crowd rushes to the heaps of rocks placed in the square a few hours earlier for this very purpose. At once, a hail of projectiles falls upon the condemned woman, who, since she has been gagged, shivers under their impact without a cry. Mohsen picks up three stones and throws them at the target. Because of the tumult around him, the first two go astray, but on the third try he hits the victim flush on the head. In an access of unfathomable joy, he sees a red stain blossom at the spot where his stone has struck her. At the end of a minute, bloody and broken, the woman collapses and lies still. Her rigidity further galvanizes her executioners; their eyes rolled back, their mouths dripping saliva, they redouble their fury, as if trying to resuscitate their victim and thus prolong her torment. In their collective hysteria, convinced that they're exorcising their own demons through those of the succubus, some of them fail to notice that the crushed body is no longer responding to their attacks and that the immolated, half-buried woman is lying lifeless on the ground, like a sack of abomination thrown to the vultures.

Two

ATIQ SHAUKAT doesn't feel well. He's tormented by the need to go outside and breathe some fresh air, to find a likely wall and stretch out on it with his face to the sun. He can't stay in this rat hole one more minute, talking to himself or trying to decipher the inextricable arabesques of words inscribed on the walls of the cells. The chill inside the little jailhouse revives his old wounds; sometimes his knee gets cold and stiffens up so much it hurts him to bend it. At the same time, he has a feeling that he's becoming claustrophobic: He can't stand the darkness any longer, nor the cubbyhole that serves as his office, festooned with spiderwebs and littered with the corpses of pill bugs. He puts away his hurricane lamp, his goatskin gourd, and the velvet-draped box where he keeps a voluminous copy of the Qur'an. After rolling up his prayer mat and hanging it on a nail, he decides to leave the jailhouse. In the unlikely event that his services are needed, the militia officers know where to find him.

The prison world is getting Atiq down. During the last several weeks, he has devoted much consideration to his position as a jailer. The more he thinks about it, the less merit he finds in it, and even less nobility. This realization has put him in a state of constant rage. Every time he closes the door behind him, withdrawing from the streets and their noise, he feels as though he were burying himself alive. A fantastic fear troubles his thoughts, and then he crouches in his corner, refusing to calm down; the act of letting himself go in this way brings him a sort of inner peace. Can it be that his twenty years of war are beginning to take their toll? At forty-two, he's already worn out; he can't see the end of the tunnel, and he can't see the end of his nose, either. Little by little, he's letting himself move toward some unthinkable renunciation. He's starting to doubt the mullahs' promises, and sometimes he catches himself feeling only the vaguest dread of being struck down by a bolt of lightning.

He's lost a considerable amount of weight. Under his fundamentalist's beard, the skin of his face sags and droops; his eyes, though outlined with kohl, have lost their keenness. The darkness of the walls has got the better of his reason, and his dark employment is taking root deep in his soul. When a man spends his nights guarding condemned prisoners and his days turning them over to the executioner, he doesn't have high expectations for his leisure time. Now, completely at a loss, Atiq is unable to say whether the silence of the two empty cells or the ghost of the prostitute who was executed this morning is the reason why the jail's shadowy corners are filled with the musty reek of the next world.

He goes out into the street. A collection of urchins is stalking a stray dog, and all are yowling in a dissonant chorale. Irritated by the noise and the turmoil, Atiq picks up a stone and throws it at the boy closest to him. The boy dodges the missile impassively and continues to scream himself hoarse. He and his fellows are trying to disorient the dog, which has plainly reached the limits of its strength. Atiq realizes that he's wasting his time. The little scoundrels won't disperse before lynching the animal, thus precociously preparing themselves to lynch men.

With his key chain under his vest, he walks to the market, which is overrun with beggars and porters. As usual, an overexcited throng, in no way disheartened by the blazing heat, boils around the vendors' makeshift stalls. Potential customers examine secondhand clothes from every angle, rummage among used objects in search of no one knows what, bruise overripe fruit with their skinny fingers.

Atiq hails a young neighbor and hands him the melon he's just bought. "Take it to my house," he commands. "And don't even think about dawdling in the street," he adds threateningly, brandishing his whip.

The boy nods in reluctant compliance, tucks the

melon under his arm, and directs his steps toward a surreal jumble of hovels.

Atiq thinks first of going to visit his uncle, a shoemaker by trade. His den is located just behind a nearby pile of ruins, but Atiq promptly dismisses the idea; his uncle is among the most tireless talkers ever begotten by his tribe, and he'll keep Atiq listening until late in the night to the same old stories, endlessly reworked, about the boots the uncle made for the king's officers and the dignitaries of the former regime. At seventy years of age, half-blind and virtually deaf, Ashraf indulges in quite a bit of raving. When his customers, exhausted by his tirades, slip out of the shop, he fails to notice their absence and keeps haranguing the walls until breath fails him. Now no one has shoes made to measure anymore, and the rare, aging specimens brought to him for repair are so severely compromised that he doesn't know where to begin. Atiq's uncle Ashraf is bored, and he bores other people to death.

Atiq stands still in the very middle of the street and considers what he's going to do this evening. He can't even think about going home to face his unmade bed, the dirty dishes forgotten in the foul-smelling basins, and his wife, lying in a corner of the room with her knees pulled up to her chin, a filthy scarf on her head, and purple blotches on her face. Because of her illness, Atiq arrived at the jail late this morning and almost jeopardized the public execution of the adulteress. It was no use going to the clinic; ever since the doctor threw up his arms in a show of impotence, the nurses can't be bothered to attend to Atiq's wife anymore. Perhaps she's another reason why Atiq has suddenly stopped believing the mullahs' promises and no longer feels any particular fear of lightning bolts fired at him from out of the blue. Prostrated, moaning, contorting her body, almost mad with pain, his wife keeps him in a state of constant alert every night and dozes off only with the coming of the dawn.

Every day, in his search for concoctions that may ease her suffering, Atiq is obliged to scour the pestilential lairs of various charlatans. But neither talismanic powers nor fervent prayers have succeeded in helping the patient. Even his own sister, who had agreed to move in with them in order to give Atiq a hand, has taken refuge in the province of Baluchistan and sent no further news. Left to his own devices, Atiq has lost his ability to manage a situation that's steadily growing more and more complicated. If the doctor has thrown in the towel, what's left except for a miracle? And do miracles still have any currency in Kabul? Sometimes, when he fears his nerves may crack under the pressure, Atiq clasps a *fatihah* in his trembling hands and implores Heaven to call back his wife. After all, why continue to suffer when each breath you take dehumanizes you and horrifies those you love?

"Watch out!" someone shouts. "Out of the way, out of the way . . ."

Atiq has just enough time to lurch to one side to avoid being run over. A horse pulling a cart has bolted. The frantic animal charges into the market, creates the beginnings of a panic, then suddenly veers off and heads for a nearby encampment. Thrown from his seat, the driver describes a low arc and lands on a canvas tent. Amid the squealing of children and the shouts of women, the horse continues its headlong dash and disappears behind the debris of a holy shrine.

Atiq hikes up the tails of his long vest and slaps the dust off his backside.

"I really thought you were done for," remarks a man sitting at a table outside a little coffee shop.

Atiq recognizes Mirza Shah, who offers him a seat and says, "Can I buy you some tea, Warden?"

"I accept gladly," says Atiq, dropping into the proffered chair.

"You've closed up shop ahead of time."

"It's hard to be your own jailer."

Mirza Shah raises an eyebrow. "You're not going to tell me your cells are empty. No more tenants?"

"No more. The last one was stoned this morning."

"The whore? I didn't attend the ceremony, but I heard about it. . . ."

Atiq leans back against the wall, folds his hand

over his belly, and looks at the rubble of what used to be, a generation ago, one of the liveliest avenues in Kabul.

"I think you look very sad, Atiq."

"Really?"

"In fact, it's the first thing one notices about you. As soon as I saw you, I said to myself, Tsk, tsk! That poor devil Atiq, all is not well with him."

Atiq shrugs his shoulders. Mirza Shah was his childhood friend. The two of them grew up together in a poverty-stricken part of town, where they went to the same places and knew the same people. Their parents worked in a little glassware factory and had worries enough without taking care of them. So, naturally, Mirza enlisted in the army at the age of eighteen, while Atiq worked as an apprentice truck driver before trying out a fantastic number of insignificant jobs, all of which reimbursed him by day for what the nights stole from him. The two friends dropped out of each other's sight until the day the Russians invaded Afghanistan. Mirza Shah was one of the first soldiers to desert his unit and join the mujahideen. His courage and his commitment quickly raised him to the rank of *tej*. Atiq met him again at the front and served for a while under his command until an artillery shell broke the momentum of Atiq's jihad. Atiq was evacuated to Peshawar; Mirza continued to make war with extraordinary zeal. After the retreat of the Soviet forces, he was offered several positions of responsibility within the administration, but he declined them all. Politics and power held few charms for him. Thanks to his connections, he was able to set up a variety of small enterprises that served as cover for his parallel investments, notably in contraband goods and the drug traffic. The rise of the Taliban cramped his style without necessarily dismantling his networks. He was happy to sacrifice a few exhausted buses and sundry other bagatelles for the good cause, contributed in his fashion to the messianic hooligans' war effort against his former comrades, and succeeded in preserving his privileges. Mirza knows that it's a rare pauper whose faith can stand against easy money, so he greases the palms of the country's new masters and passes peaceful days in the very eye of the storm. He's asked the jailer several times to come to work for him, but Atiq regularly sidesteps the offer; he prefers perishing by degrees in an ephemeral life to suffering torments for all eternity.

Mirza twirls his beads on one finger and stares at his old friend. The friend, embarrassed, pretends to examine his fingernails.

"What's wrong, Warden?"

"I'm asking myself the same question."

"Is whatever it is the reason why you were talking to yourself a little while ago?"

"Maybe."

"You can't find anybody to talk to?"

"Is that so necessary?"

"The way things are going for you, I'd say yes. You were so absorbed in your troubles, you didn't hear that cart coming. Right away I said to myself, Either Atiq's losing his mind or he's cooking up an imminent coup d'état. . . ."

"Watch what you're saying," Atiq interrupts, squirming a little. "Someone might take you literally."

"I'm just teasing you."

"There's no joking in Kabul, as you very well know."

In an effort to soothe him, Mirza gently taps the back of his hand. "We used to be great friends when we were children. Have you forgotten?"

"Hotheads don't have memories."

"We never hid anything from each other."

"Today, that's no longer possible."

Mirza's hand clenches. "And what has changed today, Atiq? The same weapons are in circulation, the same mugs are on display, the same dogs are barking, and the same caravans are passing through. We've always lived this way. One king left; another divinity replaced him. The logos on the coats of arms may have changed, but they entitle their owners to the same abuses. Don't delude yourself; the mental range is the same as it's been for centuries. Some people waste their time waiting to see a new era dawning on the horizon. As long as the world's been the world, there've been those who live with it and those who refuse to accept it. The wise man, of course, is the one who takes things as they come. He has understood. And you, too, Atiq, you have to understand. You're unhinged because you don't know what you want, that's all. But that's what friends are for: to help you to see clearly. If you still think of me as a friend, tell me a little about why you're in such a state."

Atiq sighs. He withdraws his wrist from under Mirza's hand, searches his eyes for some support, dithers briefly, then gives in. "My wife's sick. The doctor says her blood is breaking down very quickly and there's no cure for her disease."

At first, the notion that a man might speak of his wife in the street baffles Mirza; then, stroking his henna-colored beard and nodding, he says, "Is this not the Lord's will?"

"Who would dare stand against it, Mirza? Not me, in any case. I accept it completely, with boundless devotion, except that I'm distraught and all alone. I haven't got anyone to help me."

"But it's simple: Divorce her."

"She has no family left," Atiq naively replies, quite failing to notice the contempt darkening his friend's features. Mirza is visibly exasperated at being obliged to dwell upon so degrading a subject. "Her parents are dead; her brothers have gone their separate ways. And besides, I couldn't do that to her."

"Why not?"

"She saved my life, remember?"

Mirza throws his shoulders back, as though the jailer's reasoning has taken him by surprise. He thrusts out his lips and tucks his chin into one shoulder so that he's eyeing Atiq sideways. "Rubbish!" he exclaims. "God alone has power over life and death. You were wounded while fighting for His glory. Since He couldn't send Gabriel, He put this woman in your way. She took care of you *by the will of God.* She did nothing but submit to His will. What you did for her was a hundred times more valuable: You married her. What more could she hope for? She was three years older than you, already an old maid, with no vitality and no appeal. Can there be any greater generosity to a woman than to offer her a roof, protection, honor, and a name? You don't owe her anything. She's the one who should bow down before you, Atiq, and kiss the toes of your feet, one by one, every time you take off your shoes. She has little significance outside of what you represent for her. She's only a subordinate. Furthermore, it's an error to believe that any man owes anything at all to a woman. The misfortune of the world comes from precisely that misconception."

Mirza suddenly frowns. "You don't mean to tell me you're crazy enough to love her?"

"We've lived together for more than twenty years. That's not something one can just ignore."

Though scandalized, Mirza restrains himself and tries to go easy on this misguided friend of his childhood. "My poor Atiq, I live with four women. I married the first one twenty-five years ago, and the last one nine months ago. I feel nothing but suspicion for the lot of them, because I have never for a single moment had the impression that I understood anything at all about the way things work in their heads. I'm convinced that I'll never fully grasp how women think. It's as though their thought processes move counterclockwise. Whether you live one year or a century with a concubine, a mother, or your own daughter, you'll always feel that there's a gap somewhere, like an insidious ditch gradually cutting you off in order to expose you better to the hazards of your inattention. These creatures are intrinsically hypocritical and fundamentally unpredictable, and the more you think you're going to tame them, the less chance you have of breaking their evil spell. You can warm a viper in your bosom, but that won't make you immune to its poison. As to the number of years, however high, it can bring no peace to a household where the love of woman betrays the weakness of man."

"It's not a question of love."

"In that case, what are you waiting for? Kick her out. Divorce her and get yourself a strong, healthy virgin who knows how to shut up and serve her master without making any noise. I don't want to see you talking to yourself like a mental patient again, not in the street, and especially not on account of a woman. That would be an offense against God and His prophet."

Mirza abruptly falls silent. A young man with a faraway look and bloodless lips has just stopped beside the door of the little shop. He's tall, and thin patches of boyishly wispy beard adorn his handsome, youthful face. His hair, long and straight, falls to his shoulders, which are as narrow and fine-boned as a young girl's.

Mirza reaches over and shakes him. "What do you want?"

Attempting to concentrate, the young man brings his fingers to his temples in a gesture that further irritates Mirza. "Make up your mind. Step inside or go away. Can't you see we're talking here?"

Mohsen Ramat notices that the two individuals have whips in their hands and are preparing to lash him across the face. Walking backward and apologizing effusively, he moves away toward the tent encampment.

"Can you believe it?" Mirza asks indignantly. "Some people have no manners whatsoever."

Atiq shakes his head and mutters something. The intrusion has just brought some clarity to his thoughts. Now he's aware of how indecent such confidences as this are, and he's cross with himself for having been unable to resist the morbid compulsion to display his dirty linen on the sidewalk in front of a café. An embarrassed silence descends upon him and his childhood friend. They dare not even look at each other. One of them falls to contemplating the lines in his hands; the other pretends to be looking for the owner of the shop.

Three

MOHSEN RAMAT pushes open the door of his house with an uncertain hand. He hasn't eaten anything since this morning, and his ramblings have worn him out. In the shops, in the market, in the square, wherever he ventured, the immense weariness that he drags around like a convict's ball and chain caught up with him immediately. His only friend and confidant died of dysentery last year, and Mohsen's had a hard time finding anyone to take his place. It's difficult for a person to live with his own shadow. Fear has become the most effective form of vigilance. These days, everyone's touchier than ever before, a remark made in confidence can easily be misinterpreted, and the Taliban are indisposed to pardon careless tongues. Since people have nothing but misfortunes to share, everyone prefers to nibble at his disappointments in his own corner and thus avoid burdening himself with other people's problems. In Kabul, where pleasure has been ranked among the deadly sins, seeking any sort of solace from anyone not closely connected to you has become an exercise in futility. What lasting solace could one hope to obtain in a chaotic world bled white by a series of uncommonly violent wars, deserted by its patron saints, and given over to the executioners and the crows, in a world the most fervent prayers cannot bring to its senses?

In the room, apart from a large woven mat doing service as a rug, two ample, aging, burst ottomans, and a worm-eaten lectern that holds the book of Readings, nothing remains. Mohsen has sold all his furniture, piece by piece, to survive the various shortages. The windows in his darkened house are blocked up. Every time a Taliban passed in the street, he would order Mohsen to repair the broken panes without delay, along with the rickety shutters, lest the glimpse of a woman's unveiled face offend some unsuspecting passerby. Since Mohsen couldn't afford these improvements, he covered the windows with canvas curtains, and now the sun no longer visits him at home.

He leaves his shoes on the little flight of steps and collapses on one of the ottomans. A woman's voice from behind a curtain at the end of the hall asks, "Can I bring you something to eat?"

"I'm not hungry."

"Perhaps a little water?"

"If it's cold, I won't say no."

Tinkling sounds come from the next room; then the curtain is drawn aside, revealing a woman beautiful as the dawn. She places a small carafe in front of Mohsen and sits down on the other ottoman, facing him. Mohsen smiles. He always smiles when his wife shows herself to him. She is sublime, her freshness never fades. Despite the rigors of her daily life, despite her mourning for her city, which has been turned over to the obsessions and follies of men, not a single wrinkle marks Zunaira's face. It's true that her cheeks have lost their former translucence and the sound of her laughter is seldom heard, but her enormous eyes, as brilliant as emeralds, have kept their magic intact.

Mohsen brings the little carafe to his lips.

His wife waits until he finishes drinking, then clears the carafe away. "You seem exhausted," she says.

"I walked a lot today. My feet are on fire."

Zunaira brushes her husband's toes with her fingertips, then begins gently massaging his feet. Mohsen leans back on his elbows, abandoning himself to his wife's delicate touch.

"I waited for you at lunch," she says.

"I forgot."

"You forgot?"

"I don't know what came over me today. I've never had this feeling before, not even when we lost our house. It was as though I'd passed out, yet I was still wandering around, groping my way along. I couldn't recognize any of the streets I was on. I walked up and down them, but it seemed that I wasn't able to cross them. It was truly strange. I was in a kind of fog. I couldn't remember the way to where I was going, and I didn't know where I wanted to go."

"You must have been in the sun too long."

"No, it wasn't sunstroke."

Suddenly, he reaches for his wife's hand, compelling her to stop the massage. Bemused by the desperate force of the grip on her wrist, Zunaira lifts her bright eyes and looks him in the face.

Mohsen hesitates a moment, then asks in a toneless voice, "Have I changed?"

"Why are you asking me that?"

"I'm asking you if I've changed."

Zunaira furrows her splendid brow and reflects. "I don't understand what it is you want me to talk about."

"About me—what else? Am I still the same man, the one you preferred over all others? Have I kept the same habits, the same ways? Do you think my reactions are normal? Do I treat you with the same affection?"

"It's certainly true that many things around us have changed. Our house was bombed. Our relatives and friends aren't here anymore—some of them have even left this world. You've lost your business.

My career has been taken away from me. We don't have enough to eat anymore, and we've stopped making plans for the future. But we're together, Mohsen. For us, that's what has to count. We're together so that we can support each other. It's up to us, to us alone, to keep hope alive. One day, God will remember us. He'll see that the horrors we're subjected to every day haven't diminished our faith, that we haven't failed in our duty, that we deserve His mercy."

Mohsen releases his wife's wrist and runs his fingers along her cheekbone. It's an affectionate gesture, and she leans into his caress.

"You're the only sun I have left, Zunaira. Without you, my night would be darker than the deepest darkness and colder than the grave. But, for the love of God, if you find that I'm changing toward you, if I'm becoming mean or unjust, please tell me. I feel that things are escaping me, I don't think I'm in control of myself anymore. If I'm going crazy, help me to be aware of it. I'm willing to fail everyone else's expectations, but I can't let myself do you any harm, not even inadvertently."

Zunaira clearly senses the depth of her husband's distress. To prove to him that he's done nothing wrong in her eyes, she rests her cheek against his diffident palm. "We're living through some difficult times, my dear. We moan and groan so much, we've lost the idea of tranquillity. When there's a lull all of a sudden, it terrifies us, and we grow suspicious of things that pose no threat."

Mohsen gently withdraws his fingers from under his wife's cheek. His eyes mist over; he has to stare at the ceiling and struggle mightily to contain his emotion. His Adam's apple panics inside his skinny throat. So great is his remorse that a trembling begins in his cheekbones and spreads out in waves, all the way to his lips and his chin. "I did something unthinkable this morning," he declares.

Zunaira freezes, alarmed by the trouble she sees in his eyes. She tries to take his hands; he holds them up in front of his chest like a man warding off an attack.

"I can't believe it," he mutters. "How did it happen? How could I?"

More and more intrigued, Zunaira sits up straight. Mohsen starts panting. His chest rises and falls at a frightening rate. Though the words horrify him, he tells his tale: "A prostitute was stoned in the square. I don't know how, but I joined the crowd of degenerates who were clamoring for her blood. It was as though I'd been taken up by a whirlwind. I, too, wanted to be in a good position to watch the impure beast perish! And when the rain of stones began to overwhelm the demon, I found myself picking up rocks—me, too—and pelting her with them. I must have gone mad, Zunaira. How could I dare do such a thing? All my life, I've thought of myself as a conscientious objector. Some people made threats and other people made promises, but none of them ever persuaded me to pick up a weapon and kill another person. I agreed to have enemies, but I couldn't bear being the enemy of anyone else, no matter who. And this morning, Zunaira, just because the crowd was shouting, I shouted with it, and just because it demanded blood, I called out for blood, too. Since then, I can't stop looking at my hands, and I don't recognize them anymore. I walked along the streets, trying to shake off my shadow, trying to put some distance between me and what I'd done, and at every corner, at every pile of rubble, I came face-to-face with that moment of . . . of confusion. I'm afraid of myself, Zunaira. I don't have any more confidence in the man I've become."

Zunaira is petrified by her husband's story. Mohsen is not the type to bare his soul. He rarely speaks about his tribulations and almost never lets his emotions show, but a little while ago, when she detected that great pain deep inside his pupils, she knew he couldn't keep it to himself. She was braced for trouble of this kind, though not of this magnitude.

Her face pales, and for the first time her eyes, as they grow wider, lose most of their brilliance. "You stoned a woman?"

"I even think I hit her on the head."

"Mohsen, come on, you couldn't have done such a thing. That's not your way—you're an educated man."

"I don't know what came over me. It happened so fast. It was as if the crowd put a spell on me. I don't recall gathering up the stones. I only remember that I couldn't get rid of them, and an irresistible rage seemed to come into my arm. . . . What frightens me and saddens me at the same time is that I didn't even try to resist."

Zunaira stands up like one who has been knocked flat but then rises again to her feet. Weakly. Incredulous, but without anger. Her lips, which a moment ago were lush and full, have dried up. She feels around for support, finds only the end of a horizontal beam that juts out from the wall, and holds on tight. For a long time, she remains still, waiting to regain her senses, but in vain. Mohsen tries to take her hand again; she eludes him and staggers toward the kitchen amid the gentle rustling of her dress. The instant she disappears behind the curtain, Mohsen understands that he should not have confided to his wife what he refuses to admit to himself.

Four

THE SUN PREPARES to withdraw. Its beams no longer ricochet with such fury off the hillsides. But the heat-stunned old men, even as they sit in their doorways and wait impatiently for evening, know that the night will be as torrid as the day. Confined inside the vast steam room formed by its stony mountains, Kabul is suffocating. It's as though a window to hell has partially opened in the sky. The rare puffs of wind, far from refreshing or regenerating the impoverished air, mischievously fill it with eye-irritating, throat-parching dust. Atiq Shaukat observes that his shadow has lengthened inordinately; soon the muezzin will call the faithful to the Maghreb prayer. Atiq slides his whip under his belt and directs his languid steps to the neighborhood mosque, an immense, chastely whitewashed hall with a skeletal ceiling and a minaret disfigured by a bombardment.

Taliban militiamen are patrolling the perimeter

of the sanctuary in packs, seizing men who are passing by and forcing them *manu militari* to join the assembled faithful.

The interior of the sanctuary is a humming furnace. The first arrivals have stormed and occupied the worn rugs scattered on the floor near the *minbar*, the pulpit where a mullah is eruditely perusing a religious book. The less privileged are obliged to dispute the few ragged mats that are being hawked as though they were made of eiderdown. The rest of the congregation, only too happy to be out of the sun and safe from the militiamen's whips, make do with the floor, whose rugged surface makes deep imprints in their behinds.

Atiq knees aside a cluster of old men, growls at the eldest of them to flatten himself more thoroughly against the wall, and sits down with his back against a column. Once again, he glares a sullen threat at the old man, warning him to keep himself as small as possible.

Atiq Shaukat hates the elderly, especially the old folks in this part of town. Most of them are putrid untouchables, exhausted by beggary and insignificance, who spend their days chanting funereal litanies and tugging at people's clothing. In the evening, in the places where a few charitable souls put out bowls of rice for widows and orphans, these ancients forgather like ravenous dogs awaiting the signal to consume their quarry, and they feel no compunctions

about making spectacles of themselves in order to
cadge a few mouthfuls. Above all else, Atiq loathes
them for that. Every time he sees one of them in his
row at the mosque, his prayers are tinged with disgust. He dislikes the moans they emit as they grovel;
he abhors their sickly drowsiness during the sermons. As far as he's concerned, they're nothing but
cadavers, pestilential remains that the gravediggers
have unconscionably neglected, carcasses with rheumy
eyes, shattered mouths, and the stench of dying
animals. . . .

Astaghfirullah, he says to himself. My poor Atiq,
how your heart fills with venom even in the house of
the Lord. Come on, pull yourself together. Forget
about making a spectacle of your private life just
now and try not to let the Evil One contaminate your
thoughts.

He presses his hands to his temples and tries to
empty his mind; then he tucks his chin into the hollow of his throat, obstinately keeping his eyes on the
floor lest the sight of the old men disturb his con-
templation.

The muezzin goes into his alcove to call the people to prayer. In one anarchically coordinated movement, the faithful rise and start forming rows. A
small individual with pointy ears and an elvish look
pulls Atiq by the end of his vest and asks him to align
himself with the others. Irritated by this impudence,
the jailer grabs the other's wrist and twists it dis-

creetly against his side. At first, the surprised little man tries to pull his hand out of the vise that's threatening to crush it; then, having failed in the attempt, he sags, on the verge of collapsing from sheer pain. Atiq maintains the pressure for a few seconds. When he's certain that his victim is just about to start howling, he lets him go. The dwarf clutches his burning wrist before slipping it under his armpit. Then, unable to assimilate the idea that a believer could behave like this inside a mosque, he makes his way to a place in the row in front of them and doesn't turn around again.

Astaghfirullah, Atiq says to himself once more. What's happening to me? I can't bear the dark, I can't bear the light, I don't like standing up or sitting down, I can't tolerate old people or children, I hate it when anybody looks at me or touches me. In fact, I can hardly stand myself. Am I going stark raving mad?

After the prayer, he decides to wait at the mosque for the muezzin's next call. Whatever happens, he doesn't feel ready to go home *and face his unmade bed, the dirty dishes forgotten in the foul-smelling basins, and his wife, lying in a corner of the room with her knees pulled up to her chin, a filthy scarf on her head, and purple blotches on her face. . . .*

The congregation breaks up. Some go home, others stand in front of the mosque, conversing. The old

people and the other beggars, their hands already ex-
tended, crowd around the entrance to the sanctuary.
Atiq goes up to a group of disabled veterans who are
swapping war stories. The biggest of them, a kind of
Goliath entangled in his beard, is drawing some lines
in the dust with a swollen finger. The others, sitting
around him like so many dervishes, observe him in
silence. Each man is missing at least an arm or a leg,
and one of them, stationed slightly to the rear, has
lost both legs. He sits in a heap inside a custom-made
barrow designed to serve as a wheelchair. The Goliath is one-eyed, and half his face is mutilated. He
finishes his drawing, leans on his hands, and tells his
story.

"The lay of the land was just about like that," he
says. His piping voice clashes violently with his her-
culean size. "There was a mountain here, a cliff
there, and the two hills you see right here. A river
flowed here and skirted the mountain to the north.
The Soviets occupied the high ground, and their positions overlooked ours all along the line. For two
days, they kept us boxed up tight. We couldn't retreat because of the mountain. It was bare, and the
helicopters would've had no problem cutting us to
pieces. On this side, the cliff fell away into a
precipice. The river was deep and wide, and it had us
blocked on this other side. The only place to cross it
was here, where there was supposed to be a ford, and

the Russians left it open to us on purpose. The truth is, it was just a big trap. Once we sank down in there, we were done for, like drowning rats. But we couldn't stay in our position very much longer. We were low on ammunition, and there wasn't a lot to eat. Besides, the enemy had called in reinforcements, including artillery, and his guns were harassing us night and day. There was no way to get even a minute's sleep. We were in a sorry state. We couldn't even bury our dead, and they were starting to stink abominably. . . ."

The legless man, deeply offended, interrupts him. "Our dead never smelled bad," he declares. "I remember when a shell caught us by surprise and killed fourteen mujahideen at once. That's how I got my legs blown off. We were surrounded, too, just like you. We stayed in our hole for eight days. And our dead didn't even decompose. Their bodies were sprawled all around, wherever the explosion had thrown them, and they didn't smell bad, either. Their faces were serene. In spite of their wounds and the pools of blood they were lying in, you would've thought they were only sleeping."

"It was winter," the Goliath suggests.

"It wasn't winter. We were in the middle of summer. It was so hot, you could fry eggs on the rocks."

"Maybe your mujahideen were saints," says the Goliath in annoyance.

"All mujahideen are blessed by the Lord," the

legless man reminds him. The others nod in vigorous assent. "They don't stink, and their flesh doesn't decay."

"Our position stank to high heaven. Where do you suppose the smell came from?"

"From your dead mules."

"We didn't have any mules."

"In that case, there's only one other possibility: You were smelling the *Shuravi*. Those pigs would stink while getting out of a bath. I remember when we captured some of them, all the flies in the country came around for a closer look. . . ."

Pushed beyond patience, the Goliath says, "Will you let me finish my story, Tamreez?"

"I thought it was important to point out that our dead don't stink. Moreover, a kind of musky perfume surrounds them all night long, from sunset to sunrise."

The Goliath erases his dusty drawings with a forceful gesture and rises to his feet. After casting a baleful glance at the legless man, he steps over the low wall and moves off toward a tent encampment. The others remain silent until he disappears from sight, then feverishly gather around the man in the wheelbarrow.

"In any case, we all know his story by heart," says an emaciated one-armed man. "He was getting to his accident, but he was going the long way around."

"He was a great warrior," his neighbor reminds him.

"True, but he lost his eye in an accident, not in battle. And besides, I frankly wonder what side he was fighting on, if his dead stank. Tamreez is right. We're all veterans. We lost hundreds of friends. They died in our arms or before our eyes, and not a single one stank. . . ."

Tamreez fidgets in his box, adjusts the pillow under his knees—which are bound up in strips of rubber—and looks toward the group of tents, as though he fears the Goliath may return. "I lost my legs, half of my teeth, and my hair, but my memory survived intact. I remember every detail as if it were yesterday. It was the middle of the summer, and that year the heat was so bad, it drove the crows to suicide. You could see them climbing higher and higher in the sky, and then they'd let themselves drop down like anvils, with their wings pressed against their sides and their beaks pointing straight down. That's the truth—I swear it on the Holy Book. We spread out our underwear on the rocks, and they were so hot, you could hear the lice popping. It was the worst summer I ever saw. We had let our guard down, because we were positive that none of those white-arses would venture outside of their camp with the sun beating down like that. But the Russian brutes spotted our position with the help of a satellite or something of that sort. If a helicopter or a plane had flown over our hideout, we would've cleared out in a minute. But we saw nothing in the sky. Everything was totally calm, in all directions. We were in our hole, about to have lunch, when the shell came down. A dead-center bull's-eye, in the right place at the right time. Boom! I was caught in a geyser of fire and earth, and that's all I remember. When I came to, I was lying in pieces under a huge rock. My hands were all bloody; my clothes were torn and black from the smoke. I didn't understand right away. Then I saw a leg lying on the ground next to me. I didn't for a minute think it was mine. I felt nothing, I wasn't suffering at all. I was just a little groggy."

Suddenly, he turns his face toward the top of the minaret and opens his eyes wide. His lips tremble; frantic spasms convulse his cheeks. He cups his hands as if to collect water from a fountain. When he begins to speak again, his voice quavers in his throat. "And that's when I saw him. The same way I see you. It's true—I swear on the Holy Book it's true. He was up in the blue sky, flying around in circles. His wings were so white, their reflection lit up the inside of the cave. He kept on flying, round and round. I was inside a circle of absolute silence—I couldn't hear the cries of the wounded or the explosions around me—but I heard his wings. They beat the air majestically and made a silky, swishing sound. It was a magical vision. . . ."

The one-armed man asks in great agitation, "Did he come down close to you?"

"Yes," says Tamreez. "He came all the way down to me. He was in tears. His face was crimson and shining like a star."

"It was the angel of death," his neighbor declares. "It couldn't have been anything else. He always shows himself like that to the truly brave. Did he say anything to you?"

"I don't remember. He folded his wings around my body, but I pushed him away."

"Poor fool!" someone cries out. "You shouldn't have resisted him. The angel would have taken you straight to Paradise, and you wouldn't be where you are now, moldering in your wheelbarrow."

Atiq figures he's heard enough and decides to refresh his mind elsewhere. By dint of endless elaboration or unvarying repetition, according to the narrators' propensities, the stories told by the men who survived the war are well on the way to becoming genuine tall tales. Atiq sincerely thinks that the mullahs should put a stop to this. But most of all, he thinks that he can't keep walking the streets indefinitely. For a while now, he's been trying to flee his own reality, the one he can neither elaborate nor recount, certainly not to the insensitive, obtuse Mirza Shah, who's so ready to reproach people for the smattering of conscience they have left. Besides, Atiq's angry with himself for having confided in Mirza. For a glass of tea he didn't even drink! He's angry with himself for shirking his responsibilities, for having been foolish enough to believe that the best way to resolve a problem is to turn your back on it. His wife is sick. Is that her fault? Has he forgotten the sacrifices she made for him after his platoon, defeated by the Communist troops, left him for dead in a wasted village? How she hid him and nursed him for weeks on end? How she transported him on the back of a mule, through hostile territory in snowy weather, all the way to Peshawar? Now that she needs him, he shamelessly flees from her side, running to left and right behind anything that seems likely to take his mind off her.

But everything comes to an end, including this day. Night has fallen. People are going back home; the homeless are returning to their burrows. And the Taliban thugs often shoot at suspicious shadows without warning. Atiq thinks that he, too, ought to go home, where he'll find his wife in the same condition as when he left her, which is to say sick and distraught. He takes a street lined with piles of rubble, stops next to a ruin, puts an arm against the only wall left standing, plants himself fairly solidly on his haunches, rests his chin on one shoulder, and stays like that. Here and there in the darkness, where a few dim lights halfheartedly expose themselves, he hears infants crying. Their wails pierce his skull like a blade. A woman protests against the unruliness of her offspring, and a male voice quickly silences her.

Atiq straightens his neck, then his spine, and looks up at the thousands of constellations twinkling in the sky. Something like a sob constricts his throat. He has to squeeze his fists bloodless to keep from collapsing. He's tired, tired of going in circles, running after wisps of smoke, tired of these dull days trampling him down from morning till night. He can't figure out why he has survived two consecutive decades of ambushes, air raids, and explosive devices that turned the bodies of dozens of people around him into pulp, sparing neither women nor children, neither villages nor flocks, and all to wind up like this, vegetating in a dark, inhospitable world, in a completely disoriented city studded with scaffolds and haunted by doddering human wreckage—a city that mistreats him, damages him, day after day, night after night, whether he's in the company of some wretch condemned to die and awaiting her fate in his stinking jail or watching over his tormented wife, doomed to an even crueler death.

"*La hawla.*" He sighs. "Lord, if this is a test you're giving me, give me also the strength to overcome it."

Striking his hands together, he mumbles a few verses from the Qur'an and turns for home.

WHEN ATIQ OPENS the door of his house, the first thing that catches his attention is the lighted hurricane lamp. Usually at such an hour, Musarrat is in bed and all the rooms are plunged in darkness. He notices the empty pallet, the blankets neatly spread out over the mattress, the pillows propped against the wall, just as he likes them. He cocks an ear: no moaning, no sound whatsoever. He retraces his steps, observes the basins, upside down and drying on the floor, and the dishes, gleaming in their proper place. His curiosity is aroused; for months now, Musarrat has done little in the way of housework. Wasted by her illness, she spends most of her time whimpering, huddled around the pain tearing at her insides. To signal his return, Atiq coughs into his hand. A curtain is drawn aside, and Musarrat shows herself at last, haggard, crumpled, but on her feet. She can't prevent her hand from clutching the doorway for support, however, and Atiq can sense that she's battling with all her remaining strength to remain upright, as if her dignity depends on her success. He puts two fingers on his chin and raises an eyebrow, making no effort to conceal his surprise.

"I thought my sister had come back from Baluchistan," he says.

Musarrat straightens up with a jerk. "I'm not helpless yet," she points out.

"That's not what I meant. You were in a really bad way when I left this morning. Now everything's in its place and the floor's been swept. When I saw that, right away I thought my sister had come back, because we don't have anyone besides her. All the women in the neighborhood know how sick you are, but not one of them has ever dropped in to see if you could use some help."

"I don't need any of them."

"Don't be so touchy, Musarrat. Why must you turn over every word to see what's lying underneath?"

Musarrat sees that she's not improving matters between herself and her husband. She takes the hurricane lamp off the table and hangs it from a beam so it will shed more light; then she brings in a tray loaded with food. "I cut up the melon you sent me and put it on the windowsill to keep it cool," she says in a conciliatory tone. "You certainly must be hungry. I've cooked some rice the way you like it."

Atiq takes off his shabby shoes, hangs his turban and whip on a shutter knob, and sits down in front of the dented metal tray. Not knowing what to say and not daring to look at his wife, for fear of reinjuring her sensibilities, he grabs a carafe and brings it to his lips. The water runs out of his mouth and splashes his beard, which he wipes with the back of his hand before feigning interest in a barley cake.

"I made it myself," says Musarrat, watching him closely. "For you."

After a pause, he finally asks, "Why do you give yourself so much trouble?"

"I want to perform my wifely duties until the end."

"I've never demanded anything from you."

"You didn't have to."

Seated on the mat across from him, she sags a little, then fixes him with her eyes and adds, "I refuse to give up, Atiq."

"It's not a question of that, woman."

"You know how much I detest humiliation."

Atiq gives her a searching look. "Have I done something to offend you, Musarrat?"

"Humiliation isn't necessarily caused by what others think about you. Sometimes it comes from not being responsible for yourself."

"Where are you getting this nonsense, woman? You're sick, that's all. You need to rest and gather your strength. I'm not blind, and we've lived together for many years: You've never cheated anyone, not me or anybody else. You don't have to aggravate your illness just to prove something—who knows what?—to me."

"We've lived together for many years, Atiq, and for the first time I feel that I must be failing in my obligations as a wife. My husband doesn't speak to me anymore."

"I don't speak to you, it's true, but it's not because I'm rejecting you. It's just that I'm overwhelmed by this everlasting war and the squalor that spoils everything around us. I'm a part-time jailer who doesn't understand why he's agreed to stand guard over a few poor wretches instead of dealing with his own misfortune."

"If you believe in God, you must consider the fact that I've become a misfortune for you as a test of your faith."

"You're not my misfortune, Musarrat. You get these ideas all by yourself. I do believe in God, and I accept whatever trials He sends me to test my patience."

Musarrat cuts the barley cake and hands a piece to her husband. "Since we have a chance to talk for once," she murmurs, "let's try not to quarrel."

"Fine with me," Atiq says approvingly. "Since we have a chance to talk for once, let's avoid all disagreeable remarks and insinuations. I'm your husband, Musarrat. I, too, try to perform my proper conjugal duties. The problem is that I feel a little out of my depth. I don't harbor any resentment toward you; you have to know that. My silence isn't rejection; it's the expression of my impotence. Do you understand me, woman?"

Musarrat nods, but without conviction.

Atiq pokes a piece of bread into one of the dishes of food. His hand trembles; it's so difficult for him to repress the anger welling up in him that he hisses as he breathes. He hunches his shoulders and tries to regulate his breathing; then, more and more exasperated by having to explain himself, he says, "I don't like pleading my case. It makes me feel as though I've done something wrong, when I've done nothing of the kind. All I want is to find a little peace in my own home. Is that too much to ask? You're the one who gets ideas, woman. You persecute yourself, and you persecute me. It's as though you're deliberately trying to provoke me."

"I'm not trying to provoke you."

"Maybe not, but that's what it feels like. As soon as you get a little of your strength back, you stupidly wear yourself out to prove to me you're still on your feet, your illness isn't about to keep you down. Two days later, you fall to pieces, and I have to pick them up. How long do you expect this farce to last?"

"Pardon me."

Atiq heaves a sigh, moves his little bit of bread around in the cold sauce, and brings it to his mouth without raising his head.

Musarrat gathers the folds of her skirt in her arms and looks at her husband, who makes moist, unpleasant sounds as he eats. Unable to catch his eye, she contents herself with staring at the bald spot that's spreading out from the crown of his head and revealing his concave, ugly nape. She starts to talk in a despondent voice: "The other night, during the full moon, I opened the shutters so I could watch you sleep. You were slumbering peacefully, like someone with nothing on his conscience. A little smile was showing through your beard. Your face made me think of the sun coming through the clouds; it was as though all the suffering you've endured had evaporated, as though pain had never dared to touch the least wrinkle in your skin. It was a vision so beautiful, so calm, I wished the dawn would never come. Your sleep brings you to a safe place, where nothing can upset you. I sat down beside your bed. I was dying to take your hand, but I was afraid I might wake you up. So, to keep myself from temptation, I thought about the years we've shared, not often very good years, and I wondered whether, even in our best, most intense moments, we ever really loved each other. . . ."

Atiq suddenly stops eating. His fist shakes as he wipes his lips with it. He mutters a *"La hawla"* and looks his wife up and down, his nostrils twitching spasmodically. In a falsely calm voice, he asks, "What's wrong, Musarrat? You're quite talkative this evening."

"Maybe it's because we've hardly talked at all for some time."

"And what makes you so loquacious today?"

"My illness. It's a serious time, illness, a real moment of truth. You can't hide anything from yourself anymore."

"You've often been ill."

"This time, I have a feeling the disease I'm carrying around isn't going to go away without me."

Atiq pushes away his plate and backs up to the wall. "On the one hand, you cook my dinner. On the other, you prevent me from touching it. Does that seem fair?"

"Pardon me."

"You go too far, then you ask for pardon. Do you think I've got nothing else to do?"

She gets up and prepares to return behind her curtain.

"This is exactly why I tend to avoid talking to you, Musarrat. You're constantly on the defensive, like a she-wolf in danger. And when I try to reason with you, you take it badly and withdraw to your room."

"That's true," she admits. "But you're all I have. When you're annoyed at me, when you're silent and scowling, I feel as though the whole world is turning its back on me. I'd give everything I have for you. I try to deserve you at all costs, and that's why I make all these blunders. Today, I forbade myself to upset you or disappoint you, yet that's exactly what I can't stop doing."

"If that's the case, why do you keep on making the same mistake?"

"I'm afraid. . . ."

"Of what?"

"Of the coming days. They terrify me. If only you could make things easier for me."

"How?"

"By repeating to me what the doctor told you about my illness."

"Again!" Atiq exclaims in a fury.

He kicks the table over, leaps to his feet, swiftly collects his shoes, turban, and whip, and leaves the house.

Left alone, Musarrat puts her head in her hands. Slowly, her thin shoulders begin to shake.

A FEW BLOCKS away, Mohsen Ramat isn't sleeping, either. Lying on his straw mattress with his hands folded behind his head, he stares at the candle as it drips wax into its earthenware bowl and throws shadows that dance in fits and starts upon the walls. Above his head, a sagging beam in the exposed ceiling threatens to give way. Last week, a section of the ceiling in the next room came down and nearly buried Zunaira. . . .

Zunaira, who's holed up in the kitchen and taking her time about coming to bed.

Their late dinner, long since over, proceeded in silence: he was devastated; she was far away. They barely touched the food, distractedly nibbling at a bit of bread that took them an hour to get down. Mohsen felt deeply embarrassed. His account of the prostitute's execution had brought discord into his home. He'd thought that confessing his guilt to Zunaira would salve his conscience and help him get a grip on himself. Never for a moment had he imagined that his words would shock his wife so thoroughly. He tried several times to extend his hand to her, to indicate to her how sorry he was. His arm refused to obey him; it remained clamped to his side as though paralyzed. Zunaira did nothing to encourage him. She kept her head bent and her eyes on the floor, while her fingers barely brushed the edge of the little table. It took her even longer to bring a mouthful of bread to her lips than it did to take a bite of it. Distant, mechanical in her movements, she refused to rise to the surface, refused to wake up. Since neither one of them was really eating, she picked up the tray and withdrew behind the curtain.

Mohsen waited for her for a long time, then went and lay down on the pallet, where he has continued to wait for her. Zunaira has not come. He's been waiting for two hours, perhaps a little longer, and Zunaira still has not returned to his side. Not a sound comes from the kitchen to suggest that she's in there. Washing two plates and emptying a little basket of bread couldn't have taken any time at all. Mohsen sits up and lets a few moments pass before deciding he's waited long enough, he's going to see what's going on.

When he draws the curtain aside, he finds Zunaira lying on a mat with her knees pulled up to her chest and her face to the wall. He's sure she's not sleeping, but he doesn't dare disturb her. He retreats soundlessly, puts on a pair of sandals and a robe, blows out the candle, and steps outside into the street. A mass of hot, moist air presses down on the neighborhood. Here and there, in carriage entrances or in front of walls, groups of men are conversing. Mohsen doesn't deem it necessary to stray far from his house. He sits down on the front step, crosses his arms over his chest, and looks for a star in the sky. At this precise moment, a man who resembles a wild animal suddenly appears and rushes past him, striding wrathfully along the little street. A ricocheting moonbeam illuminates his hardened face; Mohsen recognizes the jailer, the man who nearly lashed him across the face with his whip outside the coffee shop a little while ago.

Five

ATIQ SHAUKAT returns to the mosque for the Isha
prayer; when it's over, he'll be the last to get to his
feet. He passes long minutes with his open hands in
a *fatihah*, reciting verses and beseeching saints and
ancestors to help him in his misfortune. Forced by
the old wounds in his knees to interrupt his prostra-
tions, he retreats into a corner cluttered with religious books and tries to read. But he can't
concentrate. The lines of the text entangle themselves before his eyes, and his head threatens to burst.
Soon the thick heat of the sanctuary obliges him to
join the faithful standing in scattered groups outside.
The old men and the beggars have disappeared, but
the disabled veterans are still there, exhibiting their
mutilations like so many trophies. The legless man is
ensconced in his barrow, listening intently to his
companions' stories, ready to assent and even readier
to object. The Goliath has returned; sitting next to a
one-armed man, he listens obsequiously as a gray-

beard relates how, with a handful of mujahideen and only one light machine gun, he succeeded in immobilizing an entire Soviet tank company.

Atiq can't put up with these preposterous feats of arms for very long. He leaves the precincts of the mosque and wanders around the city, passing through neighborhoods that look like hecatombs, wielding his whip from time to time to drive off the most relentless beggars. Suddenly, inadvertently, he finds himself standing in front of his jailhouse. He goes inside. The silence of the cells is soothing to him, and he decides to spend the night here. He gropes his way to the hurricane lamp, lights it, and lies down on the cot with his hands under his head and his eyes riveted to the ceiling. Every time his thoughts bring him face-to-face with Musarrat again, he kicks out a foot as though trying to shake them off. His anger returns, flows over him in successive waves, making his blood throb inside his temples and compressing his chest. He's angry at himself for not having dared to lance the abscess once and for all, for not having pointed out a few hard truths to his wife, who should consider herself privileged in comparison to the depraved women haunting the streets of Kabul. Musarrat is taking advantage of his patience. Her illness no longer counts as an extenuating circumstance; she has to learn how to deal with it. . . .

A huge shadow darkens the wall. Atiq gives a start and grabs his whip.

"It's only me, Nazeesh," a trembling voice reassures him.

"Nobody ever taught you to knock before you come in?" growls Atiq, furious.

"My hands are full. I didn't mean to scare you."

Atiq shines the lamp on his visitor. He's a man of about sixty, as tall as a mast, with stooped shoulders, a grotesque neck, and a swirl of wild hair topped by a shapeless head covering. His emaciated face tapers to his chin, which is prolonged by a hoary goatee, and his bulging eyes seem to spring out of his face, as though he were in the grip of some unspeakable pain.

He remains standing in the doorway, smiling indecisively, waiting for a sign from the jailer before he advances or retreats. "I saw a light," he explains. "I said, Good old Atiq, he's not doing very well, I should go and keep him company. But I haven't come with empty hands. I brought a little dried meat and some crab apples."

Atiq considers, then shrugs and points to a sheepskin on the floor. All too glad to have been granted admission, Nazeesh sits down in the indicated spot, opens a little bundle, and spreads out his bounty at the jailer's feet.

"I said to myself, Atiq was too nervous to stay

home. He wouldn't come to the jail when there aren't any prisoners, not at this time of night, unless he needed to relieve his mind. Me, too, I'm the same way. I'm not comfortable at home. My hundred-year-old father won't let up. He's lost most of his sight, he's lost the use of his legs, but his capacity for endless grousing remains intact. He's always bitching about something. Before, we could give him something to eat to shut him up. These days, we don't have very much food to sink our teeth into, and since he's lost his, there's nothing in the way of his tongue. Sometimes he starts by demanding silence, and then he's the one who can't stop talking. Two days ago, he wouldn't wake up. My daughters shook him and sprinkled water on him; he didn't move. I felt his wrist—no pulse. I put my ear against his chest—no breathing. I said, Okay, he's dead; we'll notify the family and give him a fine funeral. I left the house to tell the neighbors the news; then I went around to cousins, nephews, other relatives, and friends and announced the passing of the eldest member of the tribe. I spent the morning receiving condolences and demonstrations of sympathy. Around noon, I go back home, and who do I find in the courtyard, bitching at everybody? My father, in flesh and blood, very much alive and kicking. His mouth was open so wide, I could see his gums— they're kind of a sickly white. I think he's lost his mind. It's impossible to sit down to eat or even to go to bed with him in the house. As soon as he sees someone passing, he pounces and starts growling out insults and reproaches. Sometimes I lose *my* head, too, and I start yelling back at him. The neighbors join in, and they all believe that I'm sinning in the face of God by not being patient with my venerable sire. So in order to avoid upsetting God, I spend most of my time outside. I even take my meals in the street."

Atiq hangs his head. Sadly, Nazeesh isn't the same anymore, either. Atiq met Nazeesh a decade ago, when he was a mufti in Kabul. He wasn't an object of adulation, but hundreds of the faithful would gather to hear his Friday sermons. He lived in a big house with a garden and a wrought-iron gate, and sometimes it happened that he was invited to official ceremonies, where he received the same treatment as the notables. His sons were killed in the war against the Russians, a fact that elevated him in the esteem of the local authorities. He never seemed to complain about anything, and no one knew anybody who was his enemy. He lived a comparatively reserved life, moving from the mosque to his house, and from his house to the mosque. He read a great deal; his erudition commanded respect, even though he was seldom called upon to give his opinion. Then, without any warning, he was found one morning stalking along the avenues, wildly gesticulating, drooling, eyes bulging. The first diagnosis was that he was possessed; the exorcists, however, struggled with his demons in vain, and then he was sent for several months to an asylum. He will never return to full possession of his faculties, but sometimes, in moments of lucidity, he withdraws completely to hide his shame at what he's become. He often sits outside his front door under a faded umbrella and looks with equal indifference upon the passing people and the passage of time.

"Do you know what I'm going to do, Atiq?"

"How could I? You never tell me anything."

Nazeesh listens carefully; then, certain that there's no chance he'll be overheard, he leans toward the jailer and says in a confiding whisper, "I'm going away."

"You're going away where?"

Nazeesh looks toward the door, holds his breath, pricks up his ears. Unsatisfied, he gets up and goes out into the street to make sure there's no one around. When he returns, his pupils are sparkling with demented elation. "Damned if I know. I'm just going away, that's all there is to it. I've got everything ready—my bag, my stick, and my money. As soon as my right foot is healed, I'm turning over my ration card and all the papers I've got and then I'm going away. No thank-yous, no good-byes. I'll pick a road at random and follow it all the way to the ocean. And when I reach the shore, I'll throw myself into the water. I'm never coming back to Kabul. It's an accursed city. No one can be saved here. Too many people are dying, and the streets are full of widows and orphans."

"And Taliban, too."

Alarmed by the jailer's remark, Nazeesh jerks his head around in the direction of the door; his scrawny arm sketches a gesture of disgust and his neck grows an inch longer when he mutters, "Ah, them. They'll get theirs."

Atiq inclines his head in agreement. He picks up a slice of dried meat and examines it with a skeptical air. To prove to him that there's no risk, Nazeesh gulps down two mouthfuls. Atiq sniffs at the morsel of dessicated flesh once again before laying it aside and selecting an apple, which he bites into hungrily. "So when will your foot be healed?"

"In a week or two. And after that, without a word to anyone, I'm going to pack my things, and— *poof!*—I'll be gone in a flash, never to be seen again. I'll walk straight ahead until I keel over, without speaking to anyone, without even meeting anyone on the way. I'm going to walk and walk and walk till the soles of my feet merge with the soles of my shoes."

Atiq licks his lips, chooses another fruit, rubs it on his vest, and swallows it whole. "You're always saying you're going to leave, and you're always here."

"I've got a bad foot."

"Before this, you had a bad hip. And before that,

it was your back. And before your back, it was your eyes. You've been talking about leaving for months, and yet you're always here. You were here yesterday; you'll be here tomorrow. You're not going anywhere, Nazeesh."

"Yes I am. I'm going away. And I'll cover my tracks on every road I take. No one will know where I've gone, and even if I should want to return, I won't be able to find my way back."

"Nonsense," says Atiq. He obviously means to be disagreeable, as if frustrating the poor devil could be a way of getting revenge for his own disappointments. "You'll never leave. You're going to stay planted in the middle of the neighborhood like a tree. It's not that your roots are holding you back, it's that people like you aren't capable of venturing farther than you can see. They fantasize about distant lands, endless highways, and incredible adventures because they'll never be able to make them real."

"How do you know?"

"I know."

"You can't know what tomorrow has in store for us, Atiq. God alone is omniscient."

"You don't need a crystal ball to predict what the beggars are going to do tomorrow. Tomorrow, when the sun comes up, you'll find them in the same place, holding out their hands and whinnying, exactly as they did yesterday and the day before that."

"I'm not a beggar."

"In Kabul, we're all beggars. As for you, Nazeesh, tomorrow you'll be on your doorstep, sitting in the shade of that shitty old umbrella of yours and waiting for your daughters to bring you your wretched meal, which you'll eat at street level."

Nazeesh is upset. After all, the step he's proposed to take is one that a considerable number of people have already taken; it's happened many times over. He doesn't understand why the jailer refuses to believe that he, Nazeesh, is capable of taking it, too, and he doesn't know how to convince him otherwise. Nazeesh observes a period of silence, at the end of which he gathers up his little bundle, a sign that in his estimation the jailer is no longer worthy of his generosity.

Atiq sniggers, deliberately plucks away a third apple, and puts it aside.

"Before, when I spoke, people used to believe me," Nazeesh says.

"Before, you were in your right mind," replies the inflexible jailer.

"And now you think I'm cracked?"

"Unfortunately, I'm not the only one who thinks so."

Nazeesh shakes his chin in consternation. His hand is a little unsure as he lifts his bundle, but then he rises to his feet. "I'm going home," he says.

"Excellent idea."

With a heavy heart, he slouches to the door. Before disappearing, he confesses in a toneless voice, "It's true. Every night I say I'm going to leave, and every day I'm still here. I wonder what can be holding me back."

After Nazeesh has left, Atiq lies down on the cot again and joins his hands under his head. The ceiling in the little prison fails to inspire him with any escape fantasies, so he sits back up and clasps his face. A wave of anger mounts up to his eyeballs. With clenched fists and jaws, he rises and heads for home. If his wife persists in her role of sacrificial victim, he vows, he's going to stop treating her so gently.

Six

THE PAST NIGHT, it seems, has mellowed Zunaira's mood. This morning, she got up early, apparently reassured, and her eyes were more captivating than ever. She's forgotten our misunderstanding, Mohsen thought; soon she'll remember it and start sulking again. But Zunaira hasn't forgotten; she's simply understood that her husband is distraught, and that he needs her. To harbor ill will against him for having performed a primitive, barbarous, revolting, insane act, an act not only absurd in itself but also symptomatic of the current state of Afghanistan, an atrocious act that he regrets and suffers from as from a wound in his conscience, would only serve to render him more fragile than he already is. Things in Kabul are going from bad to worse, sliding into ruin, sweeping along men and mores. It's a chaos within chaos, a disaster enclosed in disaster, and woe to those who are careless. An isolated person is doomed beyond remedy. The other day, there was a madman in the neighborhood, screaming at the top of his lungs that God had failed. From all indications, this poor soul knew neither where he was nor how he had lost his wits. But the uncompromising Taliban, seeing no extenuating circumstances in his madness, had him blindfolded, gagged, and whipped to death in the public square.

Zunaira is no Taliban, and her husband's not mad; if he lost his way in a moment of collective hysteria, that's because the horrors of everyday life are sufficiently powerful to overwhelm all defenses, and human degeneracy is deeper than any abyss. Mohsen is behaving like other people, recognizing his distress in theirs, identifying with their degradation. His deed provides proof that everything can change, without warning and beyond recognition.

It was a long night for both of them. Petrified by his anguish, Mohsen remained outside, sitting on his stone step, until the muezzin's call. Zunaira didn't sleep a wink, either. Curled up on her mat, she sought refuge in memories of long ago, of the days when children sang in public squares now besmirched by dirt and disfigured by gallows. Not every day was a holiday, but there were no fanatics shouting "Sacrilege!" when kites fluttered in the air. Of course, Mohsen would take a certain number of precautions before allowing his hand to brush against the hand of his beloved, but such prudence only intensified the passion they felt for each other.

Traditions were traditions; one had to live with them. The necessity of discretion, far from frustrating the lovers, preserved their romance from prying eyes and increased the profound thrill they felt whenever their fingers escaped notice long enough for a magical, ecstatic touch.

They had met at the university. He was the son of a middle-class family; she was the daughter of a prominent man. Mohsen was studying political science and looking forward to a diplomatic career; Zunaira's ambition was to become a magistrate. He was a straightforward, decent, moderately religious young man; as an enlightened Muslim, she wore assertive head scarves and modest dresses, sometimes over loose trousers, and actively campaigned for the emancipation of women. Her zeal was unmatched, save by the praises heaped upon her. She was a brilliant girl, and her beauty lifted every heart. The boys never tired of devouring her with their eyes. All of them dreamed of marrying her, but Mohsen was her choice; she fell in love with him at first sight. He was courteous, and he blushed like a maiden when she smiled at him. They married very young and very quickly, as if they sensed that the worst, though yet to come to them, was already at the gates of the city.

Now Mohsen makes no effort to conceal his relief. He even tries to display it in all its fullness to his wife, so that she may judge how he languishes for her when she turns her back on him. He can't bear her not speaking to him; she's the last link that still connects him to anything in this world.

Zunaira says nothing, but her smile is eloquent. It's not the same smile her husband is used to seeing on her face; it is, however, more than enough to make him happy.

She serves him his breakfast and sits down on an ottoman, resting her folded hands on her knees. Her houri's eyes follow a wisp of smoke, then fasten on her husband's. "You got up very early," she says.

Mohsen flinches, surprised to hear her speaking to him as though nothing has happened. Her voice is gentle, almost maternal, and he deduces from it that the page has been turned.

He swallows a mouthful of bread so hastily it nearly strangles him. Wiping his lips with a hand-kerchief, he says, "I went to the mosque."

She knits her eyebrows. "At three o'clock in the morning?"

He swallows again, clears his throat, searches for a plausible explanation, and tries this: "I wasn't sleepy, so I went outside to get some fresh air."

"It really was very hot last night."

They mutually acknowledge that the humidity and the mosquitoes have been particularly disagree-able for the last few days. Mohsen adds that most of their neighbors also resorted to the street last night, escaping their baking hovels, and that some of them didn't return home until dawn. The conversation revolves around the pitiless season, the drought that has ravaged Afghanistan for years, and the diseases that are swooping down like maddened hawks on entire families. They talk about everything and nothing, without ever alluding to last night's misunderstanding or to the public executions, which are becoming more and more common.

Then Mohsen suggests, "How about taking a walk to the market?"

"We're completely broke."

"We don't have to buy anything. We can admire the heaps of old rubbish the merchants are trying to pass off as antiques."

"What will we get out of that?"

"Not much, but it's an excuse for walking."

Zunaira laughs softly, amused by her husband's pathetic sense of humor. "You don't like it here?"

Mohsen suspects a trap. With a gesture of embarrassment, he scratches the wispy hairs on his cheeks and pouts a little. "That's hardly the point. I feel like going out with you. They way we used to in the good old days."

"Times have changed."

"We haven't."

"And who are we?"

Mohsen leans back against the wall and crosses his arms over his chest. He tries to ponder his wife's question, but he finds it unreasonable. "Why are you talking nonsense?"

"Because it's the truth. We're not anything anymore. We had some privileges that we didn't know
how to defend, and so we forfeited them to the apprentice mullahs. I'd love to go out with you every
day, every evening; I'd love to slip my hand under
your arm and let you sweep me along. It would be
marvelous to stand in front of a shop window, leaning against you, or to sit at a table, just the two of us,
chatting away or making fantastic plans. But that's
no longer possible. There will always be some foul-
smelling ogre, armed to the teeth, who'll reprimand
us and forbid us to speak outdoors. Rather than be
subjected to such insults, I prefer to stay inside my
own four walls. Here at home, at least, when I see my
reflection in the mirror, I don't have to hide my
face."

Mohsen doesn't agree. He pouts harder, evokes
the shabbiness of the room they're sitting in, points to
the worn curtains, the rotting shutters, the crum-
bling walls, the sagging beams above their heads.
"This isn't our home, Zunaira. Our house, the place
where we created our own world, is gone. A shell
blew it away. What we have is just a refuge. I don't
want it to become our tomb. We've lost our fortunes;
let's not lose our way of life altogether. The only
means of resistance we have left, the only chance we
have to reject tyranny and barbarism, comes from
our upbringing and our education. We were taught
to be complete human beings, with one eye on the

Lord and the other on our own mortal nature. We've been too close to the bright lights to believe that candles are enough. We've known the joys life has to offer, and we thought them as good as the joys of eternity. We can't accept being treated like cattle."

"Isn't that what we've become?"

"I'm not sure. The Taliban have taken advantage of a period of uncertainty. They've dealt a terrible blow to people who were already defeated. But they haven't finished us off, not yet. Our duty is to convince ourselves of that fact."

"How?"

"By thumbing our noses at their decrees. We're going out. You and me. Sure, we're not going to hold hands, but there's nothing to prevent us from walking side by side."

Zunaira shakes her head. "I don't feel like coming home heartsick, Mohsen. The things that go on in the streets will just ruin my day, to no purpose. I can't come face-to-face with horrors and just keep on walking as if nothing's happened. Furthermore, I refuse to wear a burqa. Of all the burdens they've put on us, that's the most degrading. The Shirt of Nessus wouldn't do as much damage to my dignity as that wretched getup. It cancels my face and takes away my identity and turns me into an object. Here, at least, I'm *me*, Zunaira, Mohsen Ramat's wife, age thirty-two, former magistrate, dismissed by obscurantists without a hearing and without compensation, but with enough self-respect left to brush my hair every day and pay attention to my clothes. If I put that damned veil on, I'm neither a human being nor an animal, I'm just an affront, a disgrace, a blemish that has to be hidden. That's too hard to deal with. Especially for someone who was a lawyer, who worked for women's rights. Please, I don't want you to think for a minute that I'm putting on some sort of act. I'd like to, you know, but unfortunately my heart's not in it anymore. Don't ask me to give up my name, my features, the color of my eyes, and the shape of my lips so I can take a walk through squalor and desolation. Don't ask me to become something less than a shadow, an anonymous thing rustling around in a hostile place. You know how thin-skinned I am, Mohsen. I'd be angry at myself for being angry at you when you were only trying to please me."

Mohsen lifts up his hands. Zunaira feels a sudden pang for him, a man who can no longer find his place in a society turned upside down. Even in the old days, before the Taliban came, he didn't have very much drive. He was always more content to dip into his fortune than to embark on demanding, time-consuming projects. He wasn't lazy, but he detested difficulties and rarely did anything that might complicate his life. He was a man of independent means but with no tendency to excess, and he was an excellent, affectionate, considerate husband. He deprived her of nothing, refused her nothing, and yielded so easily to her requests that she often felt as if she were taking advantage of his kindness. But he was like that: openhanded, easygoing, readier to say yes than to ask himself questions. The thoroughgoing upheaval provoked by the Taliban has completely unsettled him. Mohsen's former points of reference have all disappeared, and he hasn't got the strength to invent any new ones. He's lost his possessions, his privileges, his relatives, and his friends. Reduced to the ranks of the untouchables, he spends his days stagnating, always deferring until later the promise to pull himself together.

"Well, all right," Zunaira concedes. "Let's go out. I'd rather run a thousand risks than to see you so demoralized."

"I'm not demoralized, Zunaira. If you want to stay home, that's fine with me. I promise I won't hold it against you. You're right—the streets of Kabul are hateful. You never know what's waiting for you out there."

Zunaira smiles at her husband's declarations, which are flatly belied by the miserable look on his face. "I'll go put on my burqa," she says.

Seven

ATIQ SHAUKAT shades his eyes with his hand. The fierce summer heat still has many bright days to last. Although it's not yet nine o'clock in the morning, the implacable sun beats down like a blacksmith on anything that moves. Carts and vans converge on the big bazaar in the center of town. The former are loaded with half-empty crates or shriveled produce from local truck farms; the latter carry passengers piled on top of one another like anchovies. People hobble along the narrow streets; their sandals scrape the dusty ground. Behind opaque veils, stepping like sleepwalkers, sparse flocks of women hug the walls, closely guarded by a few embarrassed males. And everywhere—in the squares, on the streets, among the vehicles, or around the coffee shops—there are kids, hundreds of little kids with snot-green nostrils and piercing eyes, disturbing, sickly, on their own, many barely old enough to walk, and all silently braiding the stout rope they'll use, someday soon, to lynch their country's last hope of salvation.

Whenever Atiq sees these children, he feels a deep uneasiness. They're invading the city inexorably, like the packs of dogs that turn up out of nowhere, feed in rubbish dumps and garbage cans, eventually colonize whole neighborhoods, and keep the citizenry at bay. The innumerable *madrassas*, the religious schools that spring up like mushrooms on every street corner, no longer suffice to hold all the children. Every day, their numbers increase and their threat grows, and no one in Kabul cares. All his adult life, Atiq has regretted that God never gave him any children; but now that the streets teem with them, he considers himself lucky. What good does it do to burden your life with a pack of brats, just so you can watch them croak little by little or wind up as cannon fodder in a war so endemic, so endless, that it has become part of the national identity?

Persuaded that his sterility is a blessing, Atiq slaps his thigh with his whip and walks toward the center of the city.

Nazeesh is dozing in the shade of his umbrella, his neck strangely twisted to one side. He's probably spent the night there, in front of his door, sitting on the ground like a fakir. When he sees Atiq coming, he pretends to be asleep. Atiq passes in front of him without saying a word. He strides on for about thirty paces, then stops, weighs the pros and cons, and retraces his steps. Watching him out of the corner of his eye, Nazeesh clenches his fists and scoots a little deeper into his corner. Atiq plants himself in front of him and crosses his arms high against his chest; then he squats down and begins drawing geometric shapes in the dirt with his fingertip. "I was rude to you last night," he acknowledges.

To enhance his impression of a beaten dog, Nazeesh presses his lips together, then says, "And I hadn't done anything to you."

"Please forgive me."

"Bah!"

"Yes, I insist. I behaved very badly toward you, Nazeesh. I was mean, and unfair, and stupid."

"But no, you were just a tiny bit disagreeable."

"I blame myself."

"That's not necessary."

"Do you forgive me?"

"Come on, of course I do. And besides, to tell the truth, some of it was my fault. I should have thought for a minute before disturbing you. There you are, in an empty jail, looking for a little peace and quiet so you can sort out your problems. And here I come, I drop in on you unannounced and talk to you about things that don't concern you. I'm the one to blame. I shouldn't have disturbed you."

"It's true that I needed to be alone."

"So it's up to you to forgive *me*."

Atiq extends his hand. Nazeesh seizes it eagerly

and holds on to it for a long time. Without letting go, he looks all around to be sure it's safe for him to speak. Then he clears his throat, but his emotion is so great that his voice comes out in an almost inaudible quaver: "Do you think we'll ever be able to hear music in Kabul one day?"

"Who knows?"

The old man strengthens his grip, extending his skinny neck as he prolongs his lamentations. "I'd like to hear a song. You can't imagine how much I'd like to hear a song. A song with instrumental accompaniment, sung in a voice that shakes you from head to foot. Do you think one day—or one night—we'll be able to turn on the radio and listen to the bands getting together again and playing until they pass out?"

"God alone is omniscient."

A momentary confusion clouds the old man's eyes; then they begin to glitter with an aching brightness that seems to rise up from the center of his being. "Music is the true breath of life. We eat so we won't starve to death. We sing so we can hear ourselves live. Do you understand, Atiq?"

"I've got a lot on my mind at the moment."

"When I was a child, it often happened that I didn't get enough to eat. It didn't matter, though. All I had to do was climb a tree, sit on a branch, and play my flute, and that drowned out my growling stomach. And when I sang—you don't have to believe me, but when I sang, I stopped feeling hungry."

The two men look at each other. Their faces are as tense as a cramp. Finally, Atiq withdraws his hand and stands up. "I'll see you later, Nazeesh."

The old man nods in agreement. Just as the jailer turns to go on his way, Nazeesh grabs his shirttail and holds him back. "Did you mean what you said yesterday, Atiq? Do you really think I'll never leave? Do you think I'm going to stay here, planted like a tree, and I'll never see the ocean or far-off lands or the edge of the horizon?"

"You're asking me too much."

"I want you to say it to my face. You're not a hypocrite; you don't care how sensitive people may be when you tell them the truth about themselves. I'm not afraid, and I won't hold it against you, but I have to know, once and for all. Do you think that I won't ever leave this city?"

"Sure you will—feetfirst. No doubt about it," Atiq says, whereupon he walks away, slapping his whip against his side.

I could have been gentler with the old man, he thinks. I could have assured him that hope is legitimate even when it's impossible. Atiq doesn't understand what came over him all of a sudden; he can't figure out why the malicious pleasure of stoking the poor devil's distress suddenly seemed more delightful than anything else. He's worried about his irresistible impulse to spoil with two words what he's spent a hundred begging for. But it's like an itch:

Even if he scratched himself bloody, he wouldn't want to be rid of it altogether. . . .

Yesterday, when he went home, he found Musarrat drowsing. Without understanding why, he purposely knocked over a stool, banged the shutters, and recited several long verses aloud before finally going to bed. When he woke up this morning, he realized what a boor he'd been. Nevertheless, he's sure he'll act the same way tonight if he goes home and finds his wife asleep.

He wasn't like this before, not Atiq. It's true, he never passed for an affable person, but he wasn't evil-tempered, either. Too poor to be generous, he prudently chose to abstain from giving, thus deliberately sparing others the duty of returning the favor. In this way, never requiring anything from anyone, he felt neither indebted nor obliged. In a country where cemeteries and wastelands compete with one another for territory, where funeral processions prolong the military convoys, war has taught him not to get too attached to anybody whom a simple caprice, a change of mood, may take away from him. Atiq has consciously enclosed himself in a cocoon, where he's exempt from making futile efforts. Acknowledging that he's seen enough of those to be moved by the plight of his fellowman, he's wary of his tendency toward sentimentality, which he looks upon as a sort of ringworm, and he limits the sorrow of the world to his own suffering. Recently, however, he's found that he's no longer content to ignore those who are close to him. Although he's made a vow to mind his own business exclusively, here he is, of all people, intentionally drawing on others' disappointments for the inspiration to master his own. Without realizing it, he's developed a strange aggressiveness, imperious and unfathomable, which seems to fit his moods. He doesn't want to be alone anymore, face-to-face with adversity; or rather, he's trying to prove to himself that burdening others will make him better able to bear the weight of his own misfortunes. Perfectly aware that he's doing Nazeesh harm, and far from feeling any remorse, he relishes his assaults as though they prove his prowess. Is that what's called "malicious pleasure"? No matter; it suits him, and even if it does him no practical good, at least he can be sure he's coming out on top. It's as though he were taking revenge on something that keeps escaping him. Ever since Musarrat fell ill, he's felt profoundly convinced that he's been cheated, that his sacrifices, his concessions, his prayers have all come to naught, that his luck will never, never, never change. . . .

"You ought to get yourself an exorcist!" a heavy voice calls out to him.

Atiq turns around. Mirza Shah is sitting at the same table as last evening, outside the coffee shop, fingering his beads. He pushes his turban back to the crown of his head and creases his brow. "You're not normal, Atiq. I told you I didn't want to see you talking to yourself in the street again. People aren't blind. They're going to decide you're a crackpot and sic their progeny on you."

"I haven't started tearing my garments yet," Atiq mutters.

"The way you're going, it won't be long."

Atiq shrugs his shoulders and continues on his way.

Mirza Shah takes his chin in his fingers and shakes his head. Certain that the jailer is going to start gesticulating again before he reaches the end of the street, Mirza watches Atiq until he's out of sight.

Atiq is furious. He's got a feeling that the whole city is spying on him, and that Mirza Shah is his chief persecutor. He lengthens his stride, determined to get away from Mirza's table as quickly as he can. He's convinced that his friend is watching him, ready to hurl another rude remark in his direction. He's so enraged that he collides with a couple on the street corner, banging first into the woman, then stumbling against her companion, who must cling to the wall to keep from falling over backward.

Atiq picks up his whip, pushes aside the man, who's trying to pull himself upright, and hastily disappears.

"A genuine lout," grumbles Mohsen Ramat as he dusts himself off.

Zunaira aims a few blows at the bottom of her

burqa. "He didn't even apologize," she says, amused by the expression on her husband's face.

"Are you all right?" he asks.

"He gave me a little scare, but that's all."

"Well then, it could be worse."

They readjust their clothing. Mohsen's movements display his irritation, while Zunaira chuckles under her mask. Mohsen perceives his wife's smothered laughter. He mutters for a moment, but then, mollified by her good humor, he bursts out laughing, too. A club immediately comes down on his shoulder.

"Do you think you're at the circus?" A Taliban police agent, his milky eyes bulging out of a face scorched red by the summer sun, is shouting at him.

Mohsen tries to protest. The club whirls in the air and strikes him in the face. "No laughing in the street," the police agent insists. "If you have any sense of shame left, you'll go home and lock yourself inside."

Pressing one hand to his cheek, Mohsen quivers with rage.

"What's the matter?" asks the Taliban agent, taunting him. "You want to gouge my eyes out? Come on, let's see what kind of guts you've got, girl-face!"

"Let's go," Zunaira entreats Mohsen, pulling him by the arm.

"Don't touch him, you! Stay in your place!" the thug yells, thwacking her across the hip. "And don't speak in the presence of a stranger."

Attracted by the commotion, other agents approach in a group, whips at the ready. The tallest of them strokes his beard with a mocking look and asks his colleague, "Is there a problem?"

"They think they're at the circus."

The tall one stares at Mohsen. "Who's that woman?"

"My wife."

"Then lead her like a man. And teach her to stand aside when you're talking with a third person. Where are you going like this?"

"I'm taking my wife to her parents' house," replies Mohsen, lying.

The Taliban agent scrutinizes him intensely. Zunaira feels that her legs are about to give way. A panicky fear seizes her. Deep in her heart, she begs her husband not to lose his composure.

"You'll take her to her parents later," the tall agent decides. "For now, you're going to join the congregation in the mosque over there. In about fifteen minutes, Mullah Bashir is going to preach a sermon."

"I'm telling you that I have to accompany my—"

Two whips interrupt him. They land simultaneously, one on each shoulder.

"I tell you that Mullah Bashir is going to preach in

ten minutes, and you talk to me about walking your wife to her parents' house. What exactly do you have inside your skull? Am I supposed to believe that you attach more importance to a family visit than to a sermon from one of our most eminent learned men?"

With the tip of his whip, he raises Mohsen's chin, forcing him to look him in the eye, then scornfully thrusts him back. "Your wife will wait for you here, by this wall, out of the way. You'll take her home later."

Mohsen raises his hands in a gesture of capitulation. After a furtive glance at his wife, he directs his steps to a green-and-white building, around which other police agents and militiamen are intercepting pedestrians and compelling them to join the faithful who are waiting to hear Mullah Bashir's words.

Eight

"THERE IS NO DOUBT," says Mullah Bashir over his goiter. His ogreish finger slashes the air like a saber.

Elephantine and domineering, he pulls at the cushion he's sitting on, adjusting it amid the creaking of the platform that serves as his rostrum. His massive face seems to burst from his stringy beard. His alert eyes, twinkling with lively, intimidating intelligence, sweep the assembly. "No doubt about it, my brothers. It's as true as the sun rising in the east. I have consulted the mountains and examined the signs in the heavens, in the waters of the rivers and the ocean, in the branches of the trees, and in the ruts in the roads; and they all affirm that the long-awaited Hour has arrived. You need only listen, only take heed, and you will hear everything on this earth, every creature, every murmuring sound, telling you that the moment of glory is within our reach, that the Imam El-Mehdi is among us, that our path is bathed in light. Those who would doubt this for a second are none of ours. The Devil dwells in them, and Hell will find inextinguishable fuel in their flesh. You will hear them for all eternity, bewailing their failure to seize the chance that we offer them on a silver platter: the chance to join our ranks, to place themselves once and for all in the shelter of the Lord."

He strikes the floor sharply with his finger. Again his flaming eyes subdue his audience, petrifying them in a sidereal silence. "Though they implore us for millions of years on end, we shall remain deaf to their pleas, just as they are deaf today to the voice of their salvation."

Mohsen Ramat takes advantage of some stirring in the front rows to cast a look over his shoulder. He sees Zunaira sitting on the steps of a ruin across from the mosque, waiting for him. A Taliban thug with a rifle slung across his back approaches her. She rises, pointing at the mosque with a timid hand. The thug looks in the direction indicated, nods, and withdraws.

Mullah Bashir drums on the floor, demanding close attention. "Henceforth, there is no doubt. The Word of righteousness resounds in the four corners of the earth. The Muslim peoples are gathering their forces, and gathering their most deeply held convictions. Soon there will be but one language on earth, but one law, one sole command." Brandishing a Qur'an, he cries out, "*This!* The West has perished; it no longer exists. It proposed a model to fools, and that model has failed. What is that model? Exactly what kind of emancipation does it offer? What does it consider modern? The amoral societies it has set up, where profit takes precedence over all else? Where scruples, piety, and charity count for nothing? Where values are exclusively financial? Where the rich become tyrants and the wage earners slaves? Where business takes the place of the family, isolates the individual, subjugates him, then dismisses him without further ado? Where women willingly give themselves over to vice? Where men marry one another? Where bodies are sold and bought openly, for all to see, without provoking the least reaction? Where entire generations are penned up in primitive existences, reduced to marginalization and impoverishment? Is that the model they're so proud of, the basis of their success? No, true believers, it is futile to build monuments on shifting sands. The West is finished, it's over and done with, its rising stench smothers the ozone layer. It is a world of lies. What you may think you discern in it is nothing but an illusion, an absurd, insubstantial phantom collapsed amid the rubble of its own flimsiness. The West is a hoax, an enormous farce, a dissolving dream. Its pseudoprogress is a flight forward, its colossal facade a masquerade. Its zeal betrays its panic. It stands at bay; it's caught like a rat in a trap. When it lost its faith, it lost its soul, and we will not help it to regain either one. It thinks that its economy is strong enough to keep it safe; it thinks it can impress us with its cutting-edge technology and intercept our prayers with its satellites; it thinks it will dissuade us with its aircraft carriers and its gimcrack armies. And it forgets that those who have chosen to die for the glory of the Lord cannot be impressed; that even though our radar may fail to detect stealth bombers, nothing escapes the eyes of the Lord!"

His fist violently strikes the floor. "And who would dare to measure himself against the Lord's wrath?"

A voracious smile curls his lips, and he wipes away the froth that has gathered in the corners of his mouth. Gently, he shakes his head; then, with his index finger, he begins pounding the floor again, as though determined to punch a hole in it. "We are God's soldiers, my brothers. Victory is our vocation; Paradise is our caravansary. Should one of us succumb to his wounds, he will find a throng of houris, beautiful as a thousand suns, waiting to welcome him. *Never believe that those who have given their lives in the Lord's cause are dead; for indeed they have not died. They are alive; they live with their Master, who showers them with His blessings.* . . . As for those who are martyrs to the cause of Evil, they will depart from the Calvary of this earth only to abide in Gehenna forever. Like the carrion that they are, their corpses will rot on the battlefields and in the memories of the survivors. They will have no right either to the Lord's mercy or to our pity. And nothing will prevent us from purifying the land of the *mumineen*, so that from Jakarta to Jericho, from Dakar to Mexico City, from Khartoum to São Paulo, from Tunis to Chicago, cries of triumph shall ring out from the minarets. . . ."

"*Allahu akbar!*" one of the mullah's companions bursts out.

"*Allahu akbar!*" the assembly roars in response.

WHEN SHE HEARS the thunderous clamor in the mosque, Zunaira jumps. Thinking that the sermon is over, she gathers up the skirts of her burqa and waits for the congregation to come out; but not so much as a shadow emerges from the sanctuary. Quite the contrary, in fact: the Taliban police continue to intercept passersby and whip them toward the green-and-white building, where the holy man, galvanized by his own words, begins to speak with renewed vigor. From time to time, his voice rises to such a pitch that the police outside surrender to its spell and forget to discipline the curious onlookers. Even the children, wild-eyed and clothed in rags, catch themselves listening to the preacher for a few moments before they dash off, squealing, into the teeming alleyways around the mosque.

It must be ten o'clock, and the sun can hold on no longer. The air is heavy with dust. Mummified under her veil, Zunaira is suffocating. Anger knots her stomach and obstructs her throat. A mad desire to lift the cloth in search of a hypothetical breath of fresh air intensifies her nervousness. But she does not even dare to wipe her dripping face on her burqa. Like a lunatic in a straitjacket, she stays where she is, slumped on her steps, sweating in the heat, listening to her breathing quicken and her blood beat in her temples. All of a sudden, she's outraged at herself for being there, sitting like a forgotten sack on the threshold of a ruin, attracting curious attention from passing women and contemptuous glances from the Taliban agents. She feels like a suspicious object exposed to every sort of interrogation, and this feeling torments her. She's overcome with shame. The urge to flee—to return home at once and slam the door behind her and never leave her house again—convulses her mind. Why did she agree to go along with her husband? What did she expect to find in the streets of Kabul except insults and squalor? How could she have consented to put on this ludicrous outfit, this getup that annihilates her, this portable tent that constitutes her degradation and her prison, with its webbed mask over her eyes like the kaleidoscopic grillwork over a window, its gloves, which take away her sense of touch, its weight of injustice? Exactly what she feared has come to pass. She knew, before she set out, that her rashness was going to expose her to the most detestable fact of her existence, to the constraint that even in her dreams she refuses to accept: the forfeiture of her rights. It's an incurable wound, a disability nothing can compensate for, a trauma beyond rehabilitation or therapy. She cannot resign herself to it without sinking into self-disgust, and Zunaira perceives that disgust quite clearly: It's an inner ferment; it sears her guts and threatens to consume her like a burning pyre. She feels its heat at the core of her being. Perhaps that's why she's sweating and suffocating under her burqa, why her parched throat seems to be disgorging an odor of cremation onto her palate. An irrepressible rage constricts her chest, bruises her heart, and swells the veins in her throat. Her vision clouds; she's on the verge of bursting into tears. With a mighty effort, she clenches her fists to stop her hands from shaking, straightens her back, and concentrates on bringing her breathing under control. Slowly, she ratchets her anger down, one notch at a time, and empties her mind of thought. She must suffer patiently; she must hold on until Mohsen comes back. One mistake, one protest, and she'll expose herself uselessly to the zeal of the Taliban.

MOHSEN RAMAT must admit that Mullah Bashir is powerfully inspired. Carried away by his diatribe, the mullah interrupts his rhetorical flights only to pound the floor or bring a small carafe to his burning lips. He's been speaking for two hours now, impassioned, gesticulating, and his saliva is as chalky white as his eyes. His taurine breathing, rumbling like a tremor in the earth, resonates throughout the room. The turbaned faithful in the front rows are unaware of the stifling heat. Literally enthralled by the holy man's verbiage, they listen openmouthed, unquenchably thirsty for the flood of words cascading down on them. Behind the first rows, opinions are divided; the mullah's prolixity instructs some and bores others. Many in the congregation, here against their will and displeased at having to neglect their business, wring their hands and shift about continually. An old man has fallen asleep; a Taliban agent prods him with his cudgel. Barely awake, the poor devil bats his eyes like a man who can't recognize his surroundings. Then he wipes his face with the palm of his hand, yawns, relaxes his birdlike neck, and goes back to sleep. Mohsen lost the thread of the sermon some time ago, and now the mullah's words have stopped reaching him altogether. He can't stop casting anxious glances over his shoulder at Zunaira, who's sitting motionless on the steps across the street. He knows she's suffering behind her curtain, both from the heat and from the mere fact of being there, an unmoving anomaly among all the passersby, she who detests making a spectacle of herself. He looks over at her, hoping she can make him out in this mob of stony-faced, incongruously silent individuals. Can

she possibly understand how much he regrets his in-
sistence on going out for a little stroll? In a city
where things move about frantically without ever
really advancing, their walk has taken a turn for the
worse. Something tells him that Zunaira will hold it
against him. She's sitting there in a rigid crouch, like
a wounded tigress compelled to go on the attack and
gathering herself to spring. . . .

A whip hisses past his temple. "You're looking the
wrong way," a Taliban agent reminds him.

Mohsen complies and, with a heavy heart, turns
his back on his wife.

When the sermon is over, the faithful in the first
rows rise euphorically to their feet and rush upon the
holy man, striving to kiss the hem of his garment or
a part of his turban. Mohsen must wait until the Taliban agents give the congregation permission to leave
the mosque. When he finally manages to break free
of the jostling throng, Mohsen finds Zunaira dazed
by the sun. She has the impression that the world has
grown darker, she hears the ambient sounds spin and
slow down, and it's hard for her to get to her feet.

"You don't feel well?" Mohsen asks her.

She finds the question so daft that she doesn't
deign to answer it. "I want to go home," she says.

Leaning against the remains of an entryway, she
tries to recover her senses, then starts to walk, stag-
gering along with blurred eyes and a boiling head.
Mohsen tries to support her, but she pushes him

away roughly. "Don't touch me!" she cries out in a strangled voice.

Mohsen feels his wife's cry as a sharp pain, like the one he felt a couple of hours ago, when two whips lashed him across the shoulders at the same time.

Nine

In a desperate effort to avoid a huge boulder, the driver gives the steering wheel a violent jerk and sends the car swerving and skidding along the shoulder of the road. The defective brakes can't slow the big 4 × 4, which bounces down an incline amid a burst of deafening pops from the shock absorbers before coming to a miraculous stop at the edge of a crevasse. Imperturbable, Qassim Abdul Jabbar merely shakes his head. "Are you trying to kill us, or what?"

The driver gulps as he realizes that one of his front wheels is about four inches from the precipice. Daubing his forehead with the tail of his turban, he mutters an incantation, puts the vehicle in reverse, and backs up.

"Where did that fucking rock come from?" the driver asks.

"Maybe it's a meteorite," says Qassim ironically.

The driver looks around, searching for a clue that might explain how the boulder could have rolled into the middle of the road. As he gazes up at the nearest ridge, he sees an old man climbing up the hillside. The driver furrows his brow. "Isn't that Nazeesh up there?"

Qassim follows the man's eyes. "I'd be surprised if it was."

The driver squints, concentrating on the ragged creature clambering up the dangerous slope. "If that's not Nazeesh, it must be his twin brother."

"Stop worrying about him and try to get me home in one piece."

The incorrigible driver nods and launches the 4 × 4 at full speed down the uneven road. Just before it curves around a hillock, he takes a last look at the rearview mirror, convinced that the old man in question is indeed the simpleminded graybeard who occasionally comes prowling around the little prison house where Atiq Shaukat spends so much of his time.

Exhausted, his throat burning and his calves knotty with pain, Nazeesh collapses on the crest of the ridge. Supporting himself on all fours, he tries to catch his breath, then lies down on his back and lets himself spin into vertigo. The sky, which seems within reach of his hand, inspires him with a rare sense of lightness; he has the sensation of emerging from a chrysalis, of slipping like a wisp of smoke through the mesh of his body. He stays that way for a while, lying on the ground with his chest heaving and his arms flung out in a cross. When the rhythm of his breathing slows to normal, he sits up and puts his drinking gourd to his lips. Now that he's conquered the mountain, there's nothing to stop him from taking on the horizon. He feels capable of walking to the ends of the earth. Proud of his exploit, unthinkable for a man of his age, he shakes his fist in the air and casts his vengeful eyes over Kabul, the old sorceress, lying there at his feet in the grip of her torments, twisted, disheveled, flat on her stomach, her jawbones cracked from eating dirt. Once upon a time, her legend rivaled those of Samarkand and Baghdad, and when her kings ascended to the throne, they immediately began dreaming of empires vaster than the firmament. . . . Those days are gone, Nazeesh thinks bitterly; you can't bring them back by circling around their memory. For Kabul has a horror of memory. She has put her history to death in the public square, sacrificed the names of her streets in horrific bonfires, dynamited her monuments into smithereens, and canceled the oaths her founders signed in their enemies' blood. Today, Kabul's enemies are her own offspring. They have disowned their ancestors and disfigured themselves in order to resemble no one, especially not those creatures who wander about like submissive ghosts bowed under the Taliban's contempt and the anathema of their holy men.

A stone's throw away, a monitor lizard surveys his realm from atop a rock, his long tail lying at his side like a saber. Of course! A truce among predators is a serious miscalculation. And in Afghanistan, whether you're a member of a tribe or a part of the fauna, whether you're a nomad or the guardian of a mosque, you never feel really alive unless you're close to a weapon. And so the big monitor is standing guard; he sniffs the air, on the lookout for traps. Now, Nazeesh does not want to hear any more talk about battles, sieges, swords, or rifles, nor has he any desire to expose himself further to the menaces of street urchins. He's decided to turn his back on the clamorous gunfire, to go and commune with himself on some wild, unspoiled beach, to see the ocean close-up. He *wants* to go to the country he's seen in fantastic daydreams, the one he's built with his sighs and his prayers and his dearest wishes—a country where the trees don't die of boredom, where the paths wander and drift like birds, where no one will look askance on his resolve to journey to the immutable lands from which he will never return. He gathers seven stones. For a long time, he glares tauntingly at the city, where his eyes can find no landmark. Suddenly, his arm uncoils and he throws his missiles as far as he can, determined to ward off ill fortune and to stone the Evil One in his tracks.

The 4 × 4 pitches madly on the unpredictable road. The recent near-fatal skid has done nothing to calm the driver. Qassim Abdul Jabbar clings to the door on his side and suffers in silence. Ever since they left Qassim's tribal village, the young chauffeur has done just as he pleased. Like most combat soldiers, he's learned to drive on the job, and he fails to notice the damage he's doing to the vehicle. As far as he's concerned, you judge an engine's worthiness according to the speed you can wrench out of its innards, a little like the way you treat a disobedient horse. Qassim, convinced that nothing he can say will have any effect on the stubborn young man, braces himself in his seat and tries to withdraw his mind from his present circumstances. He thinks about his tribe, which the war has severely reduced, about the widows and orphans, whose numbers have grown beyond the outer limits of the tolerable, about the livestock, which the harsh seasons have decimated, about his dilapidated village, where he saw no reason to linger for any length of time. Had it been up to him, he would never have set foot there again. But his mother died a few days ago and was buried yesterday. He arrived too late for the funeral services, so he contented himself with a brief period of meditation at her grave. A few minutes of silence and a verse from the Qur'an were sufficient. Then he slipped a bundle of banknotes inside his father's vest and ordered the driver to take him back to Kabul.

"We could have spent the night," the driver says, as if he were reading Qassim's thoughts.

"Why?"

"So we could rest. We didn't even have anything to eat."

"There was nothing to do up there."

"But you were with your family."

"So what?"

"Well, I don't know. If I were you, I would've stayed awhile. How many weeks has it been since the last time you went back to your village? It's been months, maybe even years."

"I don't feel comfortable in the village."

The driver nods, accepting this explanation, but he doesn't give it much credence. He watches his passenger out of the corner of his eye, thinking that Qassim is behaving quite peculiarly for someone who has just lost his mother. The young man falls silent while successfully negotiating a curve, then picks up the conversation again. "One of your cousins told me your mother was a saint."

"She was a good woman."

"Are you going to miss her?"

"Possibly, but I can't see how. She was a deaf-mute. I remember very little about her, to tell you the truth. Besides, I left home when I was quite young. At the age of twelve, I was already running from one frontier to the other, earning my bowl of rice. I seldom went back home. One Ramadan out of every three. The result was that I didn't know the deceased as well as I should have. For me, she was the woman who brought me into the world—period, new paragraph. She had fourteen kids. I was the sixth, and the least interesting. I was sullen and unapproachable, more likely to fight than cry. I thought there were too many people in the shack, and not enough ambition. Then again, my late mother was astonishingly reserved. The old man loved to say that he married her because she never questioned his orders. That made him laugh his head off. Quite a joker, the old man. A little slow on the uptake, but not demanding and never ever abusive. He had no reason to be. On the rare occasions when there was a domestic quarrel, it was conducted in complete silence, and he was too amused to lose his temper. . . ."

Qassim's reminiscences fill his eyes with a distant shimmer. He purses his lips and stops talking. He's not sad; rather, he's disappointed, as if his memories have unexpectedly upset him. After a long silence, he clears his throat, turns his whole body around to the left, and adds, "Maybe she was a saint. Why not, after all? She heard no evil and spoke no evil."

"So she was blessed."

"Well, I wouldn't go that far. She was a placid person, she had no enemies, and she led an uneventful life. For me, the epitome of her was her smile, which was always the same, except that it was bigger when she was contented and smaller when she was upset. If I left home too young, that was surely the reason. Talking to her was like talking to a wall."

The driver leans his head out of the window and spits. His saliva whirls in the flying dust before landing on his beard, which he wipes with the back of his hand. Then, in a curiously cheerful tone, he says, "I never knew my mother. She died giving birth to me. She was fourteen. My old man, who had barely reached puberty himself, was grazing the flock a few steps away, a bit lost in childish daydreams. When my mother started groaning, he didn't panic. Instead of going to fetch the neighbors, he tried to take care of her himself. Like a grown-up. Things went wrong very fast. He kept trying, and here I am. He doesn't know how I survived and, what's worse, he can't understand why my mother died on him. It still preys on his mind, after so many years and four marriages. . . . My mother suffered a lot before she passed away. I never knew her, but she's always there at my side. I swear to you, sometimes I can feel her breath on my face. I'm on my third marriage in less than a year."

"Because of her?"

"No, my first two wives were disobedient. They weren't very energetic, and they asked too many questions."

Qassim fails to see the connection. He rests his head on the back of his seat and stares up at the interior light. Another curve, and then—Kabul! Huddled amid the wreckage of her avenues, she seems at best a tragic joke, but in the background, like a raptor waiting for its quarry, looms the sinister prison of Pul-e-Sharki. Qassim's eyes gleam with a peculiar light. If he never misses an opportunity to accompany condemned wretches to the foot of the scaffold, it's precisely because he wishes to draw the mullahs' attention to himself. He was an exceptional combat soldier, and he has gained a commendable reputation as a militiaman. One day, his perseverance and dedication will induce the decision makers to appoint him commander of that fortress, the largest and most important penal institution in the country. This position will allow him to rise in status, become one of the notables, establish connections, and go into business. Then and only then will he know peace and rest from his exertions.

"So she must be in Paradise right now?"

Qassim jumps. "Who?"

"Your mother."

Qassim stares at the driver, who seems not wholly in his right mind. The young man smiles at him while steering through the middle of a web of ruts. At that instant, the road curves, they turn their backs to the city, and the fortress of Pul-e-Sharki vanishes behind a sandstone quarry.

Below them, far below them, down there where the bottom of the valley sinks beneath the deceptive waters of a mirage, a contingent of camels is climbing up the slope. Lower still, on his feet in the middle of a cemetery, Mohsen Ramat looks up at the mountainside, where the lights of a big 4 × 4 are streaking along the road.

Every morning, Mohsen comes here to look up at the taciturn peaks; he does not, however, dare to climb them. Zunaira has withdrawn into an over-whelming silence, and ever since then, Mohsen can no longer bear to go among crowds of people. When he leaves his house, he hastens to the old cemetery, where he spends hours and hours alone, far from the bazaars and their infestation of bawling vendors and armed zealots. Nevertheless, he knows that he won't draw much profit from his ascetic meditations. There's nothing to see, except for utter dereliction, and nothing to hope for. And all around him, there's the exceedingly arid landscape. It's as though the land has despoiled itself in order to heighten the distress of those who live there, trapped between the rocks and the blazing heat. The sparse strips of greenery that deign to show themselves here and there make no promise of blooming; the blades of the baked grass crumble at the least quiver. Like gigantic dehydrated hydras, the streams languish in their undone beds, with nothing but their stony bowels to offer to the sunstroke gods. What has he come looking for among these grotesque tombs, at the foot of these tac-iturn mountains?

Leading an impressive cloud of dust, the big 4 × 4 rolls through the cemetery. Qassim glances at the de-jected young man wandering among the dead. It's the same fellow he caught a glimpse of this morning, when he left for his native village. Qassim looks at him carefully for a moment, wondering what he could be doing all day long in a deserted cemetery under the scorching sun.

The driver relaxes, easing up on the accelerator as he turns into the first narrow streets of the city. The sight of groups of kids at play and clusters of old men gathered in the shade of garden fences cheers him up. He's glad to be going home. "That sure was a hell of a trip," he remarks, waving at an acquaintance in the crowd. "We spent hours jolting our vertebrae loose on bad roads, and we ate all sorts of horrible food."

"Stop whining," Qassim growls.

"After I turn off the engine, and not before," the driver says stubbornly, pulling a comical face. "What are we going to do? Shall I drop you off at home?"

"Not just yet. I need to take my mind off things. Since you won't stop griping about how I'm starving you, what do you say we go to Khorsan's and nibble on some kabob? My treat."

"I warn you, I can eat enough for four."

"I'm not afraid."

"You're a prince, boss. Thanks to you, I'm going to stuff myself until I'm sick."

Khorsan's eating place stands at one corner of a ravaged public garden, across from a bus stop. In the little square, the fumes of barbecued meat compete for the rare breezes with the clouds of smoke raised by the passing vehicles. A few customers—among them the jailer, Atiq—are sitting at the crude tables squeezed against one another under a wicker canopy. Indifferent to the sun and the squadrons of flies, the diners bestir themselves only to drive away the hungry street urchins. These children have been overexcited by the aromas coming from the grill, where Khorsan himself, his belly hanging to his knees and his beard to his navel, waves a fan to revive his coals. With the other hand, he turns the slabs of meat; when he determines that they're done, he licks his chops. The 4×4 that squeals to a stop ten feet away does nothing to disconcert him. Without taking his eye off the sizzling cutlets, he merely turns his fan toward the cloud of dust that begins to envelop his person. Qassim shows him four fingers and takes a seat on a worm-eaten wooden bench; Khorsan acknowledges the order with a movement of his head and continues his ritual with renewed application.

Atiq looks at his watch. He's clearly impatient; Qassim's arrival has driven his nervousness to new heights. What's Qassim going to think when he sees him there, eating dinner in a greasy spoon not twenty steps from his house? He hunches his shoulders and screens his face with his hand until a waiter brings him a huge sandwich bundled in wrapping paper. Atiq slips it into a plastic bag, places a few banknotes on the table, and beats a hasty retreat, without waiting for his change. Just when he thinks he's free and clear, Qassim's hand lays hold of him. "Is it me you're running from, Atiq?"

The jailer acts the part of the man who just can't believe his eyes. "Are you back already?"

"Why are you sneaking out like this? Have I given you some cause for complaint?"

"I don't follow you."

Qassim, disappointed, slowly nods his head. "Do you know what I think, Atiq? I think what you're doing is wrong. No, please, don't put on a show. It's not necessary, I assure you. I'm not going to give you a lecture. It's just that—look, I think you've changed a lot recently, and I don't like it. Normally, I wouldn't give a damn about such things, but I can't be indifferent in your case. Maybe it's because of the long years we've spent together. Sometimes we've had fun, but more often we've had to struggle against adversity. I don't like meddling in something that's not my business, but I have no qualms about telling you this: if you barricade yourself inside your worries, you're going to wind up stuck there, unable to get out."

"It's not a big deal. Sometimes I get a little depressed, that's all."

Qassim doesn't believe him and makes no attempt to hide his incredulity. He leans toward Atiq. "Do you need money?"

"I wouldn't know what to do with it."

The militiaman scratches his forehead, deep in thought, then makes a proposal. "Why don't you come and join us tonight at Haji Palwan's? Only old friends will be there. We drink tea, we talk and talk, we reminisce about the army and all our skirmishes, and we laugh at the bad old times. It'll suit you just fine, I promise. We're just a bunch of war buddies; everything's very relaxed. If you have any ideas, we'll discuss them together so you can find the right partners and get things rolling at once. You don't have to be a wizard to go into business. A little imagination, a modicum of motivation, and the locomotive starts moving down the track. If you're broke, we'll stake you and you can reimburse us later."

"It's not a question of money," Atiq declares wearily. "Money doesn't dazzle me."

"It doesn't light your way, either, as far as I can tell."

"I don't mind the dark."

"That's a statement that needs proving. For my part, I just want to tell you there's nothing wrong with going to see a friend when things are getting you down."

"Did Mirza Shah send you?"

"You see? You're wrong all down the line. I don't need Mirza Shah's advice to reach out to a colleague I'm fond of."

Atiq's neck bone protrudes as he looks down at his plastic bag. He toes a stone, unearths it, and begins digging a hole in the dirt. "May I go?" he asks in a tight voice.

"But of course, what a question!"

Atiq thanks him with a nod and starts to leave.

"There was a learned man in Jalalabad," Qassim blurts out, falling in behind Atiq. "A savant, a phenomenal sage. He had an answer for everything. No literary or scholarly allusion ever escaped him. He knew by heart every hadith in the *Six Sound Books* and all the great events that have marked the history of Islam, all Islam, from east to west. The man was astounding. If he'd lived in our times, he would've probably wound up at the end of a rope, or perhaps beheaded, because his knowledge was so great, it passed all understanding. One day, while he was teaching a class, someone came in and whispered in his ear. And all at once, the illustrious wise man turned pale. His beads slipped from his fingers. He got to his feet without a word and left the classroom. He was never seen again."

Atiq raises an eyebrow. "So what did the other person whisper to him?"

"The story doesn't say anything about that detail."

"And the moral of the story?"

"You can know all there is to know about life and mankind, but what do you really know about yourself? Atiq, my boy, don't try too hard to complicate your existence. You'll never guess what it holds in store for you. Stop filling your head with false ideas and unanswerable questions and useless reasoning. Even if you find an answer to every question today, you still won't be safe from whatever unknowable event may take place tomorrow. The learned man knew many things, but he was ignorant about the essential thing. Basically, being alive means keeping yourself ready for the sky to fall in on you at any time. If you start from the assumption that existence is only an ordeal, a test we have to pass, then you're equipped to deal with its sorrows and its surprises. If you persist in expecting it to give you something it can't give, that just proves that you haven't understood anything. Take things as they come; don't turn them into a drama. You're not piloting the ship, you're following the course of your destiny. Yesterday, I lost my mother. Today, I went to spend a few moments in silence at her grave. Now I'm at Khorsan's getting a bite to eat. I plan to go to Haji Palwan's tonight to hear what our old comrades are talking about. If some misfortune has happened since the last time I went there, it's not the end of the world. There's no more painful love than the love you feel when you're in a railroad station and you exchange glances with someone whose train is headed in the other direction."

Atiq stops walking, but he keeps his neck bowed. He reflects for a moment, then raises his chin and asks, "Is it really so obvious that I'm going through a bad time?"

"If you want my opinion, it's written all over your face."

Atiq nods and goes away.

Sadly, Qassim watches him leave. Then he scratches his head under his turban and goes back to rejoin his driver in Khorsan's little eating place.

LIFE IS NOTHING but an inexorable process of erosion, Musarrat thinks. Whether you neglect yourself or take care of yourself, it makes no sort of difference. The fact of birth dooms you to death; it's the rule. If the body could choose, people would live for a thousand years. But the will doesn't always have the power to enforce itself, and an old person's wits, however sharp, can do nothing to support his knees. The fundamental human tragedy derives from the fact that no one can outlive the most hopeless of desires, which is, moreover, the main cause of our misfortune. As for the world, isn't it a human failure, the monstrous proof of human paltriness? Musarrat has decided to face the evidence. Putting a veil over her face won't do any good. She has fought against the evil thing that's gnawing her life away; she's refused to lower her fists. But now the time has come to drop her guard, to resign herself to her fate, because that's all that's left; she's tried everything else. Her only regret is that she must falter at an age when all the chimeras have been tamed at last. At forty-five, her life is still ahead of her, but more nuanced, more care-fully measured; her dreams are less fantastic, her im-pulses more serene, and her body, when desire claws it out of its indolence, quivers with such discernment that lovemaking makes up in intensity for whatever it may have lost in freshness. The fifth decade is an age of reason, and that's an advantage when one has to negotiate challenges. In her forties, her certainty about the end she's coming to is too strong to admit a second's doubt. Musarrat has no doubts; everything will come to an end, except this certainty. There will be no miracles. The thought grieves her, but not ex-cessively. Excess would be useless, perhaps ridiculous, and surely blasphemous. Of course, she would like to make herself beautiful, to put mascara on her lashes and open her eyes so wide that nothing in Atiq's eyes could escape her notice. But such resorts are no longer possible for her. That's a hard truth to admit at forty-five years. And, alas, admitting the hard truth doesn't exempt her from very much. There is no ap-peal from the reflection she sees in the small chipped mirror: she's decomposing faster than her prayers. Her face is nothing but a fleshless skull with fur-rowed cheeks and pinched lips. Her eyes are glazed, icy, glimmering with a faint, deathly light, as though shreds of glass lie deep in her pupils. And, *my God*, her hands. Bony, covered with thin, drab skin, crum-pled like paper, they have trouble recognizing things by touch. This morning, when she finished combing her hair, she found she was holding a fistful of it in her hand. How can you lose so much hair in so little time? She wound the hair around a bit of wood and thrust it into a crack in the wall; then she slid down to the floor with her head in her hands and waited for a tear to well up and bring her back to herself. When no tear came, she crawled on all fours to her pallet. There, sitting cross-legged on the mattress, she faced the wall for a full hour. Had her strength not abandoned her, she would have spent the whole day with her back to the room. But she was felled by her own obstinacy; she lay down on the floor and fell asleep at once, her mouth open in a long, drawn-out groan.

When he found her lying in a heap on the floor, Atiq immediately feared the worst. Curiously enough, he didn't drop the package he was carrying, and his breathing was untroubled. He remained standing in the doorway, one eyebrow higher than the other, careful to make no noise. For several long minutes, he gazed at her body attentively—the hand turned toward the ceiling, the curled fingers, the open mouth, the rigid chest—looking for a sign of life. Not a hair on Musarrat's head moved. After putting his bag on a low table, Atiq swallowed hard and approached his wife's inert body. Cautiously, he knelt beside her, and at the moment when he bent over her pallid wrist to take her pulse, a soft sigh sent him lurching backward. His Adam's apple began furiously twitching. He listened carefully, imagining he had heard some ordinary rustling sound, then brought his ear close to the still face. Once again, a faint breath touched his cheek. He pressed his lips together to hold his anger in check, straightened up, and with closed eyes and clenched fists backed away until he was sitting against the wall. Sternly setting his jaw and folding his arms across his chest, he stared at the body stretched out at his feet as if he were trying to pierce it with his eyes, through and through.

Ten

MOHSEN RAMAT can take no more. The endless hours and days he regularly spends in the cemetery have exacerbated his distress. However much he may wander among the graves, he can't manage to put his ideas in order. Things are escaping him at a dizzying speed; his bearings are irretrievably lost. Instead of helping him concentrate, his isolation weakens him and magnifies his suffering. Every now and then, a mad desire to grab an iron bar and destroy everything in sight surges through him; curiously, however, as soon as he takes his head in his hands, his rage turns into an irresistible urge to burst into tears. Thus, with clenched teeth and sealed eyelids, he abandons himself to his prostration.

He thinks he's going mad.

Since the incident in the streets of Kabul, he can no longer distinguish day from night. The penalty for that accursed little outing is harsh and irreversible. If only he had listened to his wife! How could he have believed that lovers' promenades were still possible in a city that looks like a hospice for the moribund, overrun with repellent fanatics whose eyes stare out of the dark backward and abysm of time? How could he have lost sight of the horrors that punctuate daily life in a nation so contemptible its official language is the whip? He shouldn't have deluded himself. This time, Zunaira refuses to forgive and forget what happened. She holds it against him; she can't bear the sight of him, much less the sound of his voice. "For the love of God," he begged her, "don't complicate things between us." Zunaira looked him up and down, her eyes baleful behind the netting in her mask. Her chest rose, lifted by a wave of indignation. She searched for the harshest, most malicious words she could think of to tell him how terribly she suffers from what he now represents for her, how incapable she is of distinguishing him from the turbaned thugs who have transformed the streets into an arena and the days into a deathwatch, how utterly the proximity of a man, any man, both disgusts and overwhelms her. Unable to express her bitterness and her affliction with sufficient venom, she shut herself in a room and started howling like a madwoman. Terrified by his wife's deafening screams, Mohsen hurriedly left the house. Had the earth opened under his feet, he wouldn't have hesitated to jump in and let it close over him. It was horrible. Zunaira's cries echoed through the district, brought out the neighbors, stalked him like a raging flock of predatory birds. His head spun. It seemed like the end of the world.

Zunaira is no longer the woman she once was, the courageous, vivacious woman who helped him hold on, who supported him every time he stumbled. Now, having decided never again to remove her burqa, she has quite deliberately sunk into an odious world, and she doesn't seem about to emerge from it. From morning until night, she haunts the house like a ghost, obstinately wrapped up in her shroud of misfortune, which she doesn't even take off to go to bed. "Your face is the only sun I have left," Mohsen pleaded with her. "Don't hide it from me."

"No sun can stand against the night," she replied, pointedly adjusting her hood. She has worn it since they were bullied on the street the other day. It's become her fortress and her refuge, her banner and her renunciation. For Mohsen, the barrier is real: It stands between him and her; it's the symbol of the painful break that threatens to tear them apart. By denying him the sight of her, she's withdrawing from his world, renouncing it from top to bottom. The extreme position she's taken shakes his foundations. He's tried to understand, but there's nothing to understand. Does Zunaira realize how excessive her reaction is? Whether she does or not, her devotion to her own cause borders on fanaticism. When he attempts to approach her, she retreats, holding her

arms in front of her to keep him at a distance.
Mohsen doesn't insist. He lifts his own hands in a
sign of acquiescence and leaves the house, his spine
bent under a mortal load.

Ten days!

For ten days, the breach between them has grown
wider, deeper, better fortified.

For ten days, Mohsen has lived in a state of total
infirmity, in a delirium worthy of King Ubu.

Every time he enters his house, Mohsen says to
himself, This can't go on. To whom does he say these
words? Zunaira yields not so much as a square inch
of territory, nor does she lift her covering even a little. Her husband's unhappiness fails to move her;
what's worse, it increases her bitterness. She can no
longer bear his whipped-dog look or his monotonous
voice. The moment she recognizes his footsteps at
the door, she stops whatever she's doing and dashes
into the next room. Mohsen grinds his teeth to sup-
press his rage, then strikes his hands together and
turns back.

THIS EVENING, he gets the same reception. As soon
as he opens the patio door, he sees her cross the living
room, as fleeting as a hallucination, and vanish behind the curtain to her own room. During the course
of several minutes, his entire being quivers; there can
no longer be any question of walking out and slam-

ming the door behind him. Thus far, his ill-judged
departures haven't served him very well. Just the opposite, in fact—they've widened the rift that sepa-
rates him from his wife. It's time to get to the bottom
of the problem, he thinks. He dreads this moment—
Zunaira is so hardheaded, so brusque and unpredictable—but he can't prolong a steadily deterio-
rating situation.

With a deep sigh, he joins his wife in her room.

Zunaira is sitting stiff-backed on a straw mattress.
He can tell that she's as compressed as a spring, ready
to bound to her feet. Mohsen has never seen her in
such a state. Her silence is fraught, like a cloud full
of storms. Zunaira's lips are sealed; she's impossible
to fathom, and Mohsen senses that any approach to
her would be risky—not to say dangerous. Mohsen is
afraid, terribly afraid. He's like a munitions expert
defusing a bomb, fully aware that his future is hanging by a thread. Zunaira has always been difficult.
She's raw, like an open wound; she hates to suffer,
and she rarely forgives. Perhaps that's the reason
why he fears her, why he loses his composure as soon
as she frowns. His awareness of the moment's
supreme importance makes Mohsen tremble, but he
has no choice. He looks for a sign, some little clue
that might give him a modicum of confidence. Nothing. Zunaira doesn't flinch. He senses something
welling up in her behind her sphinxlike facade, as if
a pool of lava were seething deep inside her, ready to

spew forth as suddenly and violently as a volcano. Although her expression is hidden by her veil, Mohsen is convinced that the look she's giving him is charged with hatred.

"What exactly are you holding against me?" he exclaims in a harassed voice. "Are you angry because I didn't put that Taliban imbecile in his place? What could I do against him? He and his kind are the ones who make the laws. They have the power of life and death over everything that moves. Do you think I'm not bothered by the things they do? An animal, a beast of burden, would find them appalling! When I think about that militiaman, a cur unworthy to lick your footprints in the dust! My actions were abject— I'm perfectly aware of that—and I know I should have shown more pride, but by the souls of our loved ones—peace be upon them—tell me, Zunaira, what could I have done?"

Nervous and distraught, he kneels down before her and tries to take her hand. She leaps backward and gathers her shroud around her.

"This is ridiculous," Mohsen mutters. "Completely ridiculous. You treat me as though I had the plague. . . . Don't turn your back on me, Zunaira. I feel as though the whole world has a grudge against me. You're all I have. Look at my hands imploring you; see how totally lost I am without you. You're my only lifeline. You're my only connection to the world."

His eyes swell with tears. He doesn't understand how they've managed to escape his vigilance, but there they are, rolling down his cheeks, and in front of Zunaira—Zunaira, who hates to see men cry.

"I feel really bad," he says apologetically. "All of a sudden, I'm afraid of my own thoughts. I have to get a grip on myself, Zunaira. Your rejection is my worst nightmare. I don't know what to do with my days, I don't know what to do with my nights. You're my only reason for living, if living still makes any sense in this country of ours."

Once again, he tries to seize her wrist.

Zunaira cries out and rises to her feet. Panting, she says, "I've told you a hundred times not to touch me."

"What's that supposed to mean? I'm your husband."

"Prove it."

"Don't talk nonsense. What do you mean?"

Zunaira springs away from the wall and stands very close to him, thrusting her head forward so that her nose practically grazes his face. Her anger is so intense that her veil trembles before her agitated breathing. "I don't ever want to see you again, Mohsen Ramat!"

A detonation would not have shaken him so hard. Mohsen is stunned by his wife's words. At first, he's incredulous—it takes him a few seconds to absorb what he's just heard. His Adam's apple jumps up and down in his throat. The sounds of their breathing, his and Zunaira's, blend together, filling the room with an eerie humming sound. Suddenly, Mohsen gives a strange moan and punches one of the shutters so hard that his wrist cracks.

Pain distorts his features as he turns to face his wife, threatening her: "I forbid you to speak to me like that, Zunaira. You don't have the right. Are you listening to me?" he shouts, grabbing her by the throat and shaking her. "I forbid you to say that! I forbid it!"

Zunaira imperturbably loosens the fingers that are crushing her throat. *"I don't ever want to see you again, Mohsen Ramat!"* she repeats, hammering the words home, stressing every one.

In a panic, Mohsen wipes his damp hands on his sides, as if seeking to erase all traces of his brutality. He looks around, aware that the situation is getting out of hand. Pressing his palms against his temples, he tries to calm himself.

"All right," he concedes. "I think I came home too early this evening. I'll go back where I came from. If you want me to, I can spend the night out. But we absolutely must give ourselves a chance to get over this and make up. . . . I love you, Zunaira. There, that's as reasonable as I can be. I've never heard any words more terrible than the ones you just said to me. Coming from your mouth, they sound like a monstrous blasphemy. I realize now exactly how imperative it is for me to leave you alone. I'll come back tomorrow—or rather, the day after tomorrow. I don't know how I'm going to manage to hold out that long, but I'll do it. I'm prepared to do anything to save our marriage. Try to do your part, too. I love you. Whatever happens, I insist, you have to know that. It's very important. There's nothing more important."

Zunaira doesn't relent. Her lips start to move dangerously under her veil. Mohsen puts his hand over her mouth. "Not another word. You've said enough for now. Let me hope that this has just been a bad day and tomorrow everything will be the way it was before."

Zunaira steps back, away from her husband's grasping hand. "I don't think you understand," she says. "*I don't ever want to see you again, Mohsen.* Those aren't just empty words, and the passing days won't mellow them. I want you out of my life, I don't want you back in this house. And if you stay here, I'll go away."

"But why?" Mohsen protests, ripping his shirt in one violent motion and revealing his emaciated sickly white chest. "Tell me what I've done. What mistake was so grave that I deserve this fate? I feel it snapping at me, like a pack of dogs."

"It's over, Mohsen. Look, it's simple: Nothing can

ever be right between us again. The only thing I want now is for you to go away and never come back."

Mohsen shakes his head. "That's not true. I refuse to accept it."

"I'm sorry."

She starts to withdraw to her room. He snatches her back by her arm, violently yanking her toward him. "I'm still your husband, Zunaira Ramat! I didn't think it would be necessary to remind you of that, but since you insist, there it is. I'm the one in charge here. It's against our traditions for a wife to repudiate her husband. It's unheard of. And I won't permit it. I've been putting up with this for ten days, hoping that you'd come to your senses. Apparently, you're not interested in coming to your senses, and I've had it up to here!"

With a jerk, she wrenches her arm out of his grip. He catches her again, twists her wrist, and forces her to face him. "For a start, you're going to take off this fucking burqa."

"Impossible. The *Sharia* of our country requires me to wear it."

"You're going to take it off, right now."

"Ask the Taliban for permission first. Go on, let's see what kind of guts you have. Go to them and demand that they change their law, and I promise I'll take off my veil immediately. Why stay here scolding me, strong man, when you could be pulling their ears until they hear the loud, clear voice of the Lord? Since you're my very own husband, go find the miserable bastard who dared to lay a finger on your wife and chop off his hand. You want to see my face, the only sun you have left? First prove to me that a new day has dawned, that this awful night has been just a bad dream, part of some distant memory."

Mohsen crumples her veil in a concerted effort to lift it. Desperate to prevent him, Zunaira writhes and wriggles in every direction, and a fierce struggle ensues; groans and imprecations burst out against a background of heavy breathing. Mohsen clutches her frantically, tearing at her clothing, but despite the pain he's causing her, Zunaira clings to her burqa. When her husband won't let her go, she bites his shoulder, his arm, his chest, but she fails to discourage him. In a paroxysm of despair, she savagely scratches his face. Surprised to feel her nails slashing his cheekbone, Mohsen recoils. A flood of agony pours into his pupils and blinds him; his nostrils pulse with rage. One furious hand describes a dazzling arc before landing solidly on his wife's cheek. She collapses under the mighty blow.

Horrified by what he's done, Mohsen stares at his hand. How could he have dared to strike her? He doesn't remember ever laying so much as his little finger on her in anger, not one single time. He's never even imagined himself upbraiding her or reproaching her for any reason at all. He looks at his hand as if he doesn't recognize it. "What's happening to us?" he mumbles. Literally overwhelmed, shaking like a leaf, he kneels down beside his wife. "Forgive me. I didn't mean to . . ."

Zunaira pushes him away, manages to get to her feet, and staggers to the living room.

He follows after, beseeching her.

"You're nothing but a common lout," she says. "You're not much better than those raging madmen strutting around outside."

"Forgive me."

"Even if I wanted to, I couldn't."

He grabs her arm. She spins to face him all at once, gathers her last remaining strength, and catapults him toward the wall. Mohsen trips over a small carafe and falls backward. His head caroms off a projection in the wall before violently striking the floor.

When her vision clears, Zunaira realizes that her husband isn't moving. He's lying on the floor with his neck oddly twisted, his eyes wide open, and his mouth agape. A strange serenity pervades his face, barely belied by the thin trickle of blood escaping from one nostril.

"Oh my God!" she cries.

Eleven

"QASSIM ABDUL JABBAR asks you not to leave your post today," the militia soldier says. "He's got a new consignment for you."

Atiq, sitting on a stool in the entrance to the jail-house, shrugs his shoulders without taking his eyes off the trucks, loaded with soldiers, that are leaving the city in an indescribable frenzy. The drivers' bellowing and the blasts of their horns cleave the crowd like icebreakers, while groups of street kids, delighted by the upheaval the convoy is causing, run about shrieking in every direction. The news has come this morning: Commander Massoud's troops have fallen into a trap, and Kabul is sending reinforcements to annihilate them.

The militiaman also looks at the military vehicles streaming past them like the wind, leaving a storm of dust in their wake. His hand, dark with scars, instinctively squeezes the barrel of his rifle. He spits to one side and says in a grumbling voice, "It's really going to hit the fan this time. They say we've lost a lot of men, but that renegade Massoud is caught like a rat. He'll never see his goddamned Panjshir again."

Atiq picks up the glass of tea at his feet and brings it to his lips. With one eye closed against the sun, he stares at the soldier, then mutters, "I hope your Qassim isn't going to make me hang around here all day waiting for him. I've got a lot of better things to do."

"He didn't specify any time. If I were you, I wouldn't budge from here. You know how he is."

"I don't know how he is, and I don't want to find out."

The militiaman frowns, creasing his broad, prominent forehead. With a bored look in his eyes, he considers the jailer. "You're not well this morning, right?"

Atiq Shaukat's lips go slack as he sets his glass down. The other's presence irritates him. He doesn't understand why the man won't just go away now that he's delivered his message. Atiq stares at him a moment, finding his profile quite disagreeable, with his tangled beard, his flat nose, and his rheumy, inexpressive eyes.

"I can go away if you want," the soldier says, as if reading the jailer's thoughts. "I don't like to disturb people."

Atiq suppresses a sigh and turns away. The last of

the military vehicles has passed. For several minutes, they can still be heard, a distant rumble behind the ruins; then silence sets in and dampens the howling of the children. The air is still filled with dust, obscuring a section of the sky, where a flock of painfully white clouds has come to a halt. Far off, behind the mountains, one seems to hear the sound of detonations, which echoes counterfeit as they please. For ten days, sporadic firing has broken out amid general indifference. In Kabul, especially at the market and in the bazaars, the hubbub of commerce would drown out the tumult of the very worst battles anyway. Stacks of banknotes are sold at auction; fortunes are made and unmade according to mood shifts. People's eyes are fixed solely on investment and profit; news from the front is taken into consideration, but quietly, as something of a spur to business negotiations.

Atiq's sick of it. He has started seriously wondering whether he might wind up following in Nazeesh's footsteps. Apparently, the poor devil made up his mind at last; one morning not long ago, he packed his things and—*poof!*—vanished without a word to his children, who spent a week looking for him. Some shepherds claimed they'd seen the old man in the mountains, but no one took them seriously. At his age, people thought, Nazeesh wouldn't be capable of taking on even the lowest of the surrounding hills, especially in the summer heat. Atiq is nevertheless convinced that the former mullah has indeed ventured into the mountains, and that he has done so only to prove to him—to Atiq, the cruel, sardonic jailer—that he was wrong to bury him too soon.

The militiaman suddenly stoops and picks up the jailer's glass. "You're a nice fellow," he says. "I don't know what's been wrong with you lately, but that doesn't make any difference. I won't be angry if you run me off."

"I'm not running you off." Atiq sighs, watching in disgust as the other drinks from his glass. "You're the one talking about going away."

The soldier nods. He squats down with his shoulders against the wall and goes back to fingering his Kalashnikov.

After a long silence, Atiq asks him, "Whatever happened to Qaab? It's been a good while since I've seen him."

"Which Qaab? The one from the armored outfit?"

"There's only one."

Raising his eyebrows, the militia soldier turns toward the jailer. "Are you trying to make me think you don't know?"

"Know what?"

"Qaab's dead. Come on, he's been dead for more than two years."

"He's dead?"

"That's enough, Atiq. We all went to his funeral."

The jailer pouts a little, scratching his temple, but his mental efforts get him nowhere. He shakes his head in embarrassment. "How could I forget something like that?"

The militiaman, more and more fascinated, observes Atiq out of the corner of his eye. "You don't remember anything about it?"

"No."

"That's strange."

Atiq recovers his tea glass, sees that it's empty. He ponders it dreamily and places it under his stool. "How did he die?"

"You're not putting me on by any chance, are you, Atiq?"

"I assure you I'm serious."

"His tank blew up during a firing exercise. The shell had a defective charge. Instead of following proper security procedure and waiting for the official observer, Qaab immediately ejected the shell, and it exploded inside the turret. Pieces of the tank were scattered for a hundred and fifty feet all around."

"Did they find his body?"

The soldier slams the ground with his rifle butt and stands up, convinced that the jailer is making fun of him. "You aren't well today. Frankly, you're not well at all."

Whereupon he spits on the ground and goes away, cursing under his breath.

LATE IN THE AFTERNOON, Qassim Abdul Jabbar arrives in a dilapidated van. The two militiawomen accompanying him take hold of the prisoner and hurry her into the jailhouse. Giving the key a double turn, Atiq locks the new inmate inside a narrow, stinking cell at the end of the hall. His head is elsewhere, his movements mechanical; he doesn't appear to notice what's going on around him. Qassim, his arms folded across his chest and his eyes glowering down intensely from his great height, observes Atiq in silence. When the two militiawomen have climbed back into the van, Qassim declares, "At least you'll have some company."

"Is that a joke?"

"Don't you want to know what she's done?"

"What would be the good of that?"

"She killed her husband."

"These things happen."

Qassim perceives the jailer's growing disgust. This exasperates Qassim in the highest degree, but he forbids himself to yield to the temptation to put Atiq in his place. He strokes his beard as though lost in thought, then turns toward the end of the corridor and says, "She's going to stay here a bit longer than the others."

"Why?" Atiq asks in an annoyed voice.

"Because of the big rally in the stadium next Friday.

Some very high-ranking guests will be in attendance. To provide this event with some atmosphere, the authorities have decided to carry out ten or twelve public executions. Your inmate is to be included in the lot. In the beginning, the *qazi* wanted to have her shot right away. Then, since there was no woman on the program for Friday, they gave her a reprieve until then."

Atiq nods halfheartedly. Qassim puts a hand on his shoulder and says, "We waited for you at Haji Palwan's the other evening."

"Something came up."

"And the following evening, as well."

Atiq elects to beat a retreat and withdraws into the cubbyhole that serves as his office. After hesitating a moment, Qassim follows him. "Have you thought about my proposals?" he asks.

Atiq emits a snort of laughter, brief and nervous. "I'd have to have a head to be able to think about something."

"It's your fault, you refuse to open your eyes. Things are clear. All you have to do is look them in the face."

"Please, Qassim. I don't feel like going over that again."

"As you wish," Qassim Abdul Jabbar says apologetically, raising his hands in front of his chest. "I take back what I just said. But for the love of heaven, hurry up and get rid of that gloomy expression. You look like a bad omen."

Twelve

ATIQ SHAUKAT doesn't understand all at once. A kind of trigger sets off a reaction in him, and a paralyzing wave like an ice-cold shower traverses him from head to foot. The pot he's holding slips from his hands and crashes to the floor, scattering little wads of rice in the dust. For three or four seconds, he thinks he's hallucinating. Staggered by the apparition that has just struck him full force, he withdraws to his cubbyhole to recover his wits. The light from the window assaults him; the shouts of the children playing war games outside throw him into confusion. He sinks down on his camp bed, presses his fingers to his temples, and curses the Evil One repeatedly in an attempt to remove his baleful influence.

"La hawla!"

After his head has partially cleared, Atiq goes back into the hallway to get the pot. He replaces its lid, which had rolled some distance away, and picks up the clumps of rice sprinkled across the floor. As he cleans up, he cautiously lifts his eyes to the roof beam looming over the cell like a bird of evil augury, and his gaze lingers on the anemic little lightbulb, growing steadily dimmer in its ceiling socket. Screwing his courage to the sticking point, he walks back to the lone occupied cell, and there, in the very middle of the cage, the magical vision: the prisoner has removed her burqa! She's sitting cross-legged on the floor. Her elbows are on her knees, her hands are joined under her chin. She's praying. Atiq is thunderstruck. Never before has he seen such splendor. With her goddess's profile, her long hair spread across her back, and her enormous eyes, like horizons, the condemned woman is beautiful beyond imagination. She's like a dawn, gathering brightness in the heart of this poisonous, squalid, fatal dungeon.

Except for his wife's, Atiq hasn't seen a woman's face for many years. He's even learned to live without such sights. For him, women are only ghosts, voiceless, charmless ghosts that pass practically unnoticed along the streets; flocks of infirm swallows—blue, yellow, often faded, several seasons behind—that make a mournful sound when they come into the proximity of men.

And all at once, a veil falls and a miracle appears. Atiq can't get over it. A complete, solid woman? A genuine, tangible woman's face, also complete, right there in front of him? He's been cut off from such a forbidden sight for so long that he believed it had been banished even from people's imaginations. When he was a young man, just emerging from adolescence, he profaned the sanctuary of a couple of girl cousins in order to spy on them in secret, feasting his senses on their outbursts of laughter, their physical loveliness, the litheness of their movements. He'd even fallen in love with an Uzbek schoolteacher, whose endless braids made her way of walking as much of an enchantment as a mystical dance. At that impressionable age, when fables, like traditions and prejudices, pathetically live on, resisting all assaults, Atiq was convinced that he had but to dream of a girl and he would glimpse a corner of Paradise. Of course, this was not the surest way to get there, but it was the least inhuman.

Then all that came to an end; that world of bold delight is gone, broken up and crumbled away. Dreams have veiled their faces. A hood with latticed eyeholes has come down and confiscated everything: laughs, smiles, glances, dimpled cheeks, fringed eyelashes. . . .

The following morning, Atiq is still sitting in the hallway, facing the prisoner. He realizes that he's stayed up the entire night, and that he hasn't taken his eyes off her for an instant. He feels completely odd, light-headed and sore-throated. He has the sensation that he's waking up inside someone else's skin. With the force of a sudden possession, something has overwhelmed him, invaded his innermost recesses. It animates his thoughts, quickens his pulse, regiments his breathing, inhabits his least tremor; sometimes he pictures it as a reed, but rigid and unyielding, and sometimes it's like some sort of reptilian ivy, winding itself around his very existence.

Atiq doesn't even try to make sense of all this. He feels no pain, but a vertiginous, implacable sensation, an exhilaration bordering on ecstasy, overcomes him, reducing him to such a state that he even forgets to perform his morning ablutions. It's as though he were under a spell, except that this is no spell. Atiq ponders the seriousness of his impropriety, measures it, and dismisses it. He lets himself go somewhere— somewhere close and yet very far away—where he can listen attentively to his own most imperceptible pulsations while remaining deaf to the most peremptory calls to order.

"What's the matter?" Musarrat asks. "That's the fifth time you've salted your rice, and you haven't even tasted it yet. And you keep on putting the water cup to your mouth without ever taking a sip."

Atiq gazes stupidly at his wife. He doesn't seem to grasp the meaning of her words. His hands are trembling, his heart is racing, and now and again his breathing is afflicted by a kind of suffocation. On wobbly legs, his head emptied of thought, he walked home, but he can't recall how; he doesn't remember meeting anyone on the streets of his district, streets where he can't ordinarily venture without being hailed or greeted by many acquaintances. He has never before in his life known the condition in which he's been languishing since the previous evening. He's not hungry; he's not thirsty. The world around him doesn't so much as graze his consciousness. What he's experiencing is at once prodigious and terrifying, but he wouldn't be rid of it for all the gold on earth: He feels *fine*.

"What's wrong with you, Atiq?"

"I beg your pardon?"

"God be praised, you can hear. I was afraid you'd been struck deaf and dumb."

"What can you be talking about?"

"Nothing," Musarrat says, giving up.

Atiq replaces his cup on the floor, takes a pinch of salt from a small earthenware bowl, and once again begins mechanically sprinkling the white granules over his dish of rice. Musarrat puts her hand to her mouth to hide a smile. Her husband's absentmindedness amuses and worries her, but his radiant face, she must admit, is reassuring. She's rarely seen him so endearingly awkward. He looks like a child just back from a puppet show. His eyes are sparkling, dazzled from within, and his agitation is almost unbelievable in one who never shakes, except with indignation, and then only when he's repressing his anger and not threatening to destroy everything in sight.

"Eat," she urges him.

Atiq stiffens. His forehead huddles around his eyebrows. Suddenly he leaps up, slapping his thighs. "My God!" he cries out as he snatches his great bunch of keys from its designated nail. "I'm inexcusable."

Musarrat tries to get to her feet. Her thin arms give way, and she falls back onto her pallet. The effort has drained her strength; she leans against the wall, her feet out in front of her, and stares at her husband. "Now what have you done?"

Atiq feels badgered but replies nonetheless: "I just remembered—I didn't give the prisoner anything to eat."

He turns on his heels and disappears.

Musarrat remains where she is, deep in thought. Her husband has gone out without his turban, his vest, and his whip. Such a thing has almost never happened. She waits, expecting him to return for his things. Atiq doesn't return. From this, Musarrat concludes that her husband, the part-time jailer, is no longer in full possession of his faculties.

ZUNAIRA IS ASLEEP, lying on a worn blanket. The sight of her makes Atiq think of a sacrificial offering. Around her, the cell, its corners spattered with un-

equivocal stains, sways in the pulsing light of the
hurricane lamp. The night is thick, dusty, without
real depth, its busy whir clearly audible. Atiq places
a tray laden with skewered meats (bought with
money from his own pocket), a flat cake, and some
fruit on the floor of the cell. He squats down and extends an arm to wake the prisoner; his fingers hover
above the curve of her shoulder. She must regain her
strength, he tells himself. His thoughts, however, do
not suffice to activate his hand, which continues to
hesitate, suspended in the air. He creeps backward
until he's leaning against the wall. Clasping his
drawn-up legs, he wedges his chin between his
knees, then sits unmoving, with his eyes riveted on
the woman's body. Its shadow, fashioned by the
bright lamplight and cast upon the wall as upon a
canvas, delineates the landscape of a dream. Atiq is
astonished by the prisoner's composure. He doesn't
believe that tranquillity could reveal itself more
plainly anywhere else than on that face, as limpid
and beautiful as water from a spring. And that black
hair, smooth and soft, which the least impudent of
breezes would lift as easily as a kite. And those delicate, translucent houri's hands, which look as soft as
a caress. And that small round mouth... *"La
hawla,"* Atiq says, pulling himself together. He
thinks, I have no right to take advantage of the fact
that she's asleep. I must go back home; I must leave
her alone. Atiq thinks, but he does not act. He stays

where he is, squatting in the corner, his arms embracing his legs, his eyes bigger than his conscience.

"IT'S VERY SIMPLE," Atiq declares. "No words can describe her."

"Is she so beautiful as that?" Musarrat asks skeptically.

"Beautiful? The word sounds commonplace to me—it sounds banal. The woman languishing in my jail is more than that. I'm still trembling from the sight of her. I spent the night watching her sleep. Her magnificence so filled my eyes that I didn't notice the dawn."

"I hope she didn't distract you from your prayer."

Atiq lowers his head. "It's true—she did."

"You forgot to perform your *salaat*?"

"Yes."

Musarrat bursts into tinkling laughter, which quickly gives way to a succession of coughs. Atiq frowns. He doesn't understand why his wife is laughing at him, why she's not cross. It's not often that he hears her laugh, and her unusual gaiety makes their dark hovel almost habitable. Panting but delighted, Musarrat wipes her eyes, adjusts the cushion behind her, and leans back on it.

"Am I amusing you?" Atiq asks.

"Enormously."

"You think I'm ridiculous."

"I think you're fabulous, Atiq. Why would you hide such generous words from me? After more than twenty years of marriage, at last you reveal the poet who's been hiding inside you. You can't imagine how happy I am to know that you're capable of speaking from your heart. Generally, you avoid such words as though they were pools of vomit. Atiq, the man with the eternal frown, the man who could walk past a gold coin without deigning to notice it, this man has tender feelings? That doesn't simply amuse me; it revives me. I'd like to kiss the feet of the woman who's awakened such sensitivity in you in the course of a single night. She must be a saint. Or perhaps a good fairy."

"That's what I said to myself the first time I saw her."

"Then why have they sentenced her to death?"

Atiq flinches. Evidently, he hasn't asked himself this question. That's not like him at all, Musarrat thinks. Surely there must be some mistake. "How about her? What's her story?"

"I haven't spoken to her."

"Why not?"

"It isn't done. I've guarded many female prisoners awaiting execution, some of them for several days. We never exchanged a single word. It's as if you're all alone and the other person isn't there. We ignored one another completely, they in their cells and me in my hole. Tears can't do any good when a sentence of death has been pronounced. In such cases, there's no place like a prison for gathering your thoughts, so people keep quiet. Especially the night before an execution."

Musarrat seizes her husband's hand and presses it against her chest. Surprisingly, the jailer offers no resistance. Perhaps he doesn't notice. His gaze is far away, his breathing tense.

"Today I feel quite strong," she says, elated by the color in her husband's face. "If you'd like, I could fix her something to eat."

"You'd do that for her?"

"I'd do anything for you."

Thirteen

THE PRISONER pushes away her tray and wipes her lips delicately on the end of a rag. Her way of patting the corners of her mouth reveals her origins in a social rank that has been abolished and no longer exists. She has class, and she's surely well educated. Atiq scrutinizes her while pretending to examine the lines in his hand. He doesn't want to miss a single one of her movements; he wants to take in all her expressions, all her ways—of eating, of drinking, of picking up the things around her and putting them down again. As far as he's concerned, there's no doubt: This woman has been rich and distinguished, has worn silk and jewels, has doused herself with fantastic perfumes and mistreated the hearts of innumerable suitors; her face has radiated the joy of many an ardent love; her smile has soothed many a misfortune. How has she wound up here? What wretched wind has blown her into this dungeon, a woman whose eyes seem to hold the light of all the world?

Those eyes look up at him. An immense oppression crushes his chest, and he quickly turns away. When he glances at the prisoner again, he finds her staring at him with an enigmatic little smile playing on her lips. To subdue his mounting embarrassment, he asks her if she's still hungry. She shakes her head. He remembers that there are some berries on his desk, but he doesn't dare go to fetch them. To tell the truth, he doesn't *want* to go away, not even for a second. He feels *fine*, just where he is, on this side of the bars, yet at the same time so close to her that he believes he can register the beating of her pulse.

The woman's smile doesn't fade. It floats on her face like the beginnings of a dream. Is she really smiling, or is he seeing visions? Since being confined to his jail, she hasn't said a word. Silent and dignified, she encloses herself in her exile, betraying neither anxiety nor torment. She looks as if she's waiting for the sun to come up so that they can leave together, without a sound. The imminent expiration of her brief reprieve hangs over her prayers like a patient blade, but its pernicious shadow cannot reach her thoughts. She seems impregnable in her martyrdom.

"My wife prepared this meal for you," Atiq says. "You're very lucky."

What a voice! Atiq drinks it in and waits for her to expand on this subject, to speak a little about her dramatic circumstances, which he knows must be eating her up inside. He waits in vain.

After a long silence, he hears himself murmur, "He deserved to die."

Then, with increased fervor, he says, "I'd take my oath on it. A man who doesn't appreciate his good fortune has no right to any sympathy." His Adam's apple scrapes his throat as he adds, "I'm certain he was a brute. Of the worst kind. Full of himself. He couldn't have been anything else. When you don't appreciate your good fortune, you forfeit your right to it. It's obvious."

The prisoner tenses her shoulders.

As Atiq's words come faster, his voice grows steadily louder. "He abused you, isn't that right? If he didn't like some little thing you said, he rolled up his sleeves and attacked you."

She lifts her head. Her eyes remind him of jewels; her smile has become more pronounced, at once sorrowful and sublime.

"He pushed you too far, was that it? He made you suffer more than you could bear. . . ."

"He was marvelous," she says in a tranquil voice. "I'm the one who didn't appreciate my good fortune."

ATIQ IS OVERWROUGHT. He can't stand still. Ever since he came home, earlier than expected, he hasn't stopped walking back and forth in the patio, turning his eyes skyward and talking to himself.

Sitting on her pallet, Musarrat watches him without a word. This whole affair is beginning to bother her. Atiq hasn't been himself since they put that prisoner in his charge. "What's the matter?" he shouts at her. "Why are you looking at me like that?"

Musarrat thinks it would be unwise to answer him, though not so unwise as it would be to try to calm him down. Atiq looks as though that's exactly what he's waiting for, an excuse to pounce on her. His eyes are full of wrath, and his clenched knuckles are white.

He approaches her. There's a milky secretion in the corners of his mouth. "You said something?"

She shakes her head.

He puts his hand on his hip and turns toward the courtyard; then, grimacing with rage, he strikes the wall and bellows, "It was a stupid accident. It could happen to anyone. It was the kind of thing you can't anticipate, the kind of thing that takes you by surprise. Her husband tripped over a carafe and struck his head on the floor, fatally. It was as simple as that. It's a tragedy, that's true, but it was an accident. She wasn't responsible for anything, the poor woman. The *qazi* must be made to see that they were wrong to condemn her. They don't have the right to send an innocent person to her death just because she was involved in an accident. That woman didn't kill her husband. She didn't kill anyone."

Musarrat nods her head timidly. Lost in his tirade, Atiq doesn't even notice.

"I must speak to Qassim about her," he says at the end of a long monologue. "He's got influential friends and connections in high places. People will listen to him. They can't possibly let an innocent woman be executed because of a misunderstanding."

"WHAT ARE YOU talking about?" Qassim Abdul Jabbar demands indignantly. He's not best pleased with Atiq, who has disturbed him in his home about a lot of nonsense. "She's a mad bitch; she's been judged and condemned. Soon she'll be executed in the stadium. Many prestigious guests are coming to the ceremony, and she's the only woman on the entire program. Even if she were innocent, no one could do anything for her. And since she's guilty—"

"She's innocent."

"How do you know that?"

"She told me so."

"And you believed her?"

"Why shouldn't I?"

"Because she lied to you. She's an incorrigible liar, Atiq. She's taking advantage of your good nature. Don't play defense lawyer for a criminal you hardly know. You have enough problems as it is."

"She didn't kill anyone. . . ."

"Her neighbors testified against her. Their statements were categorical. That whore led her unfortunate husband a dog's life. She was constantly chasing him out of his own home. The *qazi* didn't even need to deliberate."

Qassim seizes the jailer by the shoulders and looks him right in the eye. "Atiq, my poor Atiq. If you don't get a grip on yourself right away, you're going to wind up so lost, you won't find your way home. Forget that witch. In a few days, she'll join the ones who've gone before her, and a new one will come and take her place. I don't know how she managed to bamboozle you, but if I were you, I'd try not to be fooled by the way she looks. You're the one who needs attention, not her. I warned you the other day. You spend too much time in your bad moods, Atiq, all locked up inside them. Be careful, I told you: One day, you won't be able to get out. You didn't listen to me, and what's the result? Your black moods weakened you, and when some smelly bitch appeared, all she had to do was whine and it broke your heart. Let her croak. I can assure you, she's right where she belongs. After all, she's only a woman."

Atiq is beside himself. Caught up in a whirlwind, he doesn't know where to hide his head or what to do with his hands when he catches himself cursing the whole world. He understands nothing, nothing at all. He's become someone else, he's been overwhelmed by a different person, who pummels him and submerges him, and without whom he'd feel like a cripple. How can he explain the shaking fits that make him shiver during the hottest hours of the day, or the sweats that cool him off a minute later? Never before has he lifted so much as a finger to help people in trouble, not even when a flick would have sufficed, so how can he explain his new boldness, his new ardor in this fight against the inevitable? How can he explain the impetuous wave of emotion that undoes him whenever he meets the prisoner's eyes? He has never thought himself capable of sharing any stranger's distress. His whole adult life has been based on this ambition: to be able to pass a torture victim without lingering over him, to be able to return from a cemetery with his resolutions intact. And suddenly here he is, desperately involved in the fate of a female prisoner whom no one can rescue from the shadow of the scaffold. Atiq doesn't understand why, all of a sudden, his heart is beating in another's place, nor why he has accepted so readily, from one day to the next, a change in himself of such magnitude that nothing will ever again be as it was before.

He had expected to find in Qassim Abdul Jabbar a modicum of indulgence, some inclination to leniency that would help him petition the *qazi* and induce them to reconsider their verdict. Qassim's reaction was disappointing—or rather, unforgivable; now Atiq loathes him entirely. Everything's over between them. No sermon, no holy man will reconcile them. Qassim is nothing but a brute. He has no more heart than a cudgel, no more mercy than a snake. He embodies the common evil, and he will die of it. They will *all* die of it, without exception: the *qazi*, crouched inside their venerable monstrousness; the howling fanatics, feverish and obscene, who are already making preparations to fill the stadium on Friday; the prestigious guests, who are coming to share the joy of public executions; the notables, who will applaud the implementation of the *Sharia* with the same hands that shoo flies, and wave away the lifeless remains with the same gestures that bless the grotesque zeal of the executioners. *All* of them. Including Kabul itself, the accursed city, every day more expert in killing, more dedicated to the opposite of living. In this land, the public celebrations have become as appalling as the lynchings themselves.

Atiq returns home. "I'm not going to let them murder her," he protests.

"Why are you getting yourself in such a state?" Musarrat admonishes him. "She's not the first, and she won't be the last. It's insane, the way you're acting. You have to pull yourself together."

"I don't want to pull myself together."

"You're doing yourself a useless injury. Look at you! Anyone would think you've gone crazy."

Atiq shakes a threatening finger at her. "I forbid you to call me crazy."

"Then pull yourself together, right now," Musarrat urges him again. "You're acting like someone who doesn't know where he is. And whenever I try to reason with you, you get twice as angry."

Atiq seizes her by the throat and jams her against the wall. "Stop your yapping, you old hag. I can't stand the sound of your voice any longer, or the smell of your body, either. . . ."

He lets her go.

Shocked by her husband's violence and devastated by his words, Musarrat sinks to the floor, her hands holding her bruised throat, her eyes bulging in disbelief.

Atiq makes an infuriated gesture, picks up his turban and his whip, and leaves the house.

THERE'S A HUGE CROWD at the mosque; the beggars and the disabled veterans are engaged in a bitter struggle for what little space is left in the recesses of the sanctuary.

Atiq finds the spectacle so revolting that he spits over his shoulder and decides to say his prayers somewhere else. As he moves off, he runs across Mirza Shah, who's hastening to join the faithful before the muezzin's call. He hurries past Atiq without paying him any attention. Then Mirza Shah stops, turns around, and gazes at his old friend for a long time before scratching his head under his turban and continuing on his way. Atiq is walking straight ahead, with an aggressive step and squinting eyes. He crosses streets without looking either left or right, indifferent to the blaring horns and the cries of the wagoners. Someone calls out to him from inside a small café; Atiq doesn't hear him. He wouldn't hear a thunderstorm if it should burst over his head. He hears only the blood pulsing in his temples and sees only his furies, all of them busily suffusing his mind with darkness: Qassim, making light of his torment; Musarrat, not understanding the depth of his grief; heaven, looking elsewhere; the ruins, turning their backs on him; the eager spectators, preparing to crowd the stadium on Friday; the Taliban agents, strutting along the thoroughfares; the mullahs, haranguing the crowds, shaking fingers more deadly than sabers. . . .

As Atiq slams the jailhouse door behind him, the confused sounds that have pursued him here fade away. All at once, the abyss is before him, and a silence as deep as a long fall. What's happening to him? Why not open the door again and let the sounds catch up with him, along with the twilight, the smells, and the dust? Panting, bent forward at the waist, he walks up and down the corridor. His whip slips from his hand; he doesn't pick it up. He keeps pacing, pacing, his beard pressed into the hollow of his throat, his hands behind his back. He comes to an abrupt stop, springs to the cell door, unlocks it, and resolutely yanks it open.

Frightened by the jailer's violence, Zunaira raises her arms to protect her face.

"Get out of here," he says to her. "Night is falling. Take advantage of it and run away. Get as far as possible from this city of madmen. Run as fast as you can, and whatever happens, don't look back. If you do, you'll suffer the same fate as Lot's wife."

Zunaira fails to grasp what her guard is getting at. She cowers under her blanket, certain that her hour has come.

"Please get out," Atiq implores her. "Don't stay here. Go away. I'll tell them it was my fault. I'll say I must have padlocked the chains wrong. I'm a Pashtun, like them. They'll curse me, but they won't hurt me."

"What's going on?"

"Please don't look at me like that. Put your burqa back on and leave."

"And go where?"

"Anywhere. Just don't stay here."

She hangs her head. Her hands reach for something under the blanket, something that's hard to reach and that she will not reveal. "No," she says. "I've already destroyed one household. I don't want to ruin any others."

"The worst thing that can happen to me is that I'll lose my job. Believe me, that's the least of my concerns. Please go away now."

"I have nowhere to go. Everyone in my family is either dead or reported missing. The only connection I still had disappeared through my own fault. I had a little light. I blew on it, trying to turn it into a torch, but I blew a bit too hard and put it out. Now there's nothing holding me back anymore. I can't wait to get out of here, but not in the way you propose."

"I won't let them kill you."

"We've already been killed, all of us. It happened so long ago, we've forgotten it."

Fourteen

THE DAYS PASS like indolent elephants. Atiq is tossed back and forth between feelings of inadequacy and visions of eternity. The hours of daylight are extinguished faster than drifting sparks; the nights drag themselves out, as interminable as torture. Suspended between the two extremes, he longs to tear himself apart. His unhappiness is driving him mad; there's no place that can contain him. He's seen wandering in side streets and alleyways, his eyes wild, his forehead creased and furrowed. In the jailhouse, no longer daring to venture into the corridor, he shuts himself up in his nook and hides behind the Qur'an. After a few chapters, he feels enervated, unable to breathe; he goes outside for some fresh air, and soon he's making his way through the crowds like a spirit in the underworld. Musarrat doesn't know how to help him. When he returns home, he withdraws almost immediately to his room, and there, seated before a small reading stand, he recites verse after verse from the Qur'an in a steady drone. When Musarrat looks in, she finds him buried in his torments, on the verge of fainting, his voice quavering and his hands over his ears. She sits down across from him, turns to the *fatihah*, and prays. As soon as he notices her presence, he snaps the Holy Book shut and goes back out, only to return a little later, purple-faced and gasping for breath. He hardly eats at all anymore, nor does he sleep at night, dividing his time between the prison—where he never stays long—and his room, which he abandons almost as soon as he enters. Musarrat is so dismayed by her husband's condition that it makes her forget the disease that's sapping her strength. When Atiq is late, horrible images fill her head. She can see that the jailer has lost much of his reason, and she knows that bad things happen fast.

One evening, she joins him in his room and practically snatches away the reading stand. When there's nothing between the two of them, she takes him firmly by the wrist and shakes him. "Get a grip on yourself, Atiq."

Atiq replies in a stupefied voice. "I held the door wide open for her and told her to go away. She refused to leave her cell."

"That's because, unlike you, she knows that no one can escape his own destiny. She's accepted her fate; she's resigned to it. You're the one who refuses to see things as they are."

"She didn't kill anyone, Musarrat. I don't want her to pay for a crime she didn't commit."

"You've seen many others die before her."

"Which proves that there are some things one can never get used to. I'm angry at myself, and I'm angry at the universe. How can a person accept dying because a bunch of incompetent *qazi* reached a hasty verdict? It's ridiculous. And even if she isn't strong enough to keep on fighting, I'm not going to give up. She's so young, so beautiful, so . . . gorgeously alive. Why didn't she leave when I held the door wide open for her?"

Tenderly, Musarrat lifts his chin and thrusts her hand into his tangled beard. "And you? Tell me honestly—look at me, please, and tell me, swear to me— would you have let her go?"

Atiq shivers. His eyes are dull with unbearable misery. "I've already told you: I held the door wide open for her."

"I heard you. But would you have let her go?"

"Of course."

"You would have watched her go away into the night without running after her? You would have let her disappear when you knew it would be forever and you'd never see her again?"

Atiq sags; his beard is heavy in his wife's unsteady hand. Musarrat keeps stroking his cheek. "I don't think so," she says to him.

"Then explain it to me," he moans. "For the love of the Prophet, tell me what's happening to me."

"The best thing that can happen to anyone on earth."

Atiq jerks his head up so hard that the movement ripples his shoulders. "What exactly do you mean, Musarrat? I have to understand."

She takes his face in her hands, and what she reads in his eyes is the final blow. A shudder courses throughout her body. She tries to struggle against her emotions, but in vain; two large tears form on her eyelids, then roll down her face and reach her chin before she has time to stop them.

"I think you've finally found your way, Atiq, my husband. A new day is dawning for you. Something is taking place inside you that would make you the envy of saints and kings. Your heart is being reborn. I can't really explain it to you, and besides, it's better that I don't. But I can tell you it's nothing for you to be afraid of."

"So what should I do?"

"Go back to her. Before you open the door for her, open your heart and let it speak. She'll listen, and she'll follow you. Take her by the hand and leave, both of you. Go as far as you can, and don't look back."

"You're asking me to go away, Musarrat?"

"I'd throw myself at your feet if I thought that would persuade you."

"I will not abandon you."

"I don't doubt it, but that's not the question. That woman needs you. Her life depends on your choice. Ever since you saw her, there's been a gleam in your eye. She lights you up inside. Another man in your position might go up on the roof and start singing at the top of his voice. If you're not singing, Atiq, it's because no one ever taught you how. You're happy, but you don't know it. You're even overflowing with happiness, and you don't know how to rejoice in it. All your life, you've only listened to other people— your teachers and your holy men, your leaders and your demons—and they've spoken to you of nothing but wrongs and bitterness and war. That's what your ears are filled with; that's why your hands shake. And that's why you're afraid to listen to your heart right now and seize the opportunity that's come to you at last. If we were in some other place, your distress might arouse the sympathy of everyone in the whole city. But Kabul doesn't know much about this kind of distress. Our city has renounced it, in fact, and that's the reason why nothing turns out right here, neither joys nor sorrows. . . . Atiq, my man, my husband, you've been blessed. Listen to your heart. It's the only voice that's talking to you about yourself, the only counselor that knows the real truth. Its reasons are stronger than all the reasons in the world. Trust your heart and let it guide your steps. And above all, don't be afraid. Because this evening, you of all men are the one who *loves*. . . ."

Atiq begins to tremble.

Taking his face in her hands again, Musarrat implores him: "Go back to her. There's still time. With a little bit of luck, you'll be on the other side of the mountain before the sun comes up."

"I've been thinking about doing just that for two days and two nights. I'm not sure it would be a good idea. They'd catch us and stone us to death. I don't have the right to offer her any false hopes. She's so unhappy, and so fragile. I go around and around, walking the streets, brooding over my escape schemes. But as soon as I see her calmly sitting in her corner, all my certainties fall to pieces. Then I go back out into the streets and wander some more, I come back here with my head full of plans, and as my strength comes back, I lose whatever certainty I've managed to recover. I'm completely lost, Musarrat. I don't want them *to take her away from me*, you understand? I've given them the best years of my life, my wildest dreams, my body and my soul. . . ."

And, to his wife's utter amazement, Atiq hides his head behind his knees as his shoulders shake with sobs.

ATIQ MUST GET READY. Tomorrow, Qassim Abdul Jabbar will come to fetch the prisoner and take her where gods and angels fear to tread. He changes his clothes and winds his turban tightly. His precise gestures contrast with his fixed stare. From the other side of the room, her face half hidden in darkness, Musarrat observes him. She says nothing when he passes near her and doesn't move when she hears him pull the latch open and walk out the door.

There's a full moon; things can be seen clearly, and from far away. Groups of insomniacs obstruct the doorways of various hovels; their gabbling stirs up the stridulations of the night. Behind some walls, a baby wails; its little voice slowly ascends into the sky, where millions of stars are signaling to one another.

The jailhouse is lying low, shrouded in its proper atmosphere of dread. Atiq cocks an ear, but he hears nothing except the beams cracking from the heat. He lights the hurricane lamp; his distorted shadow leaps upon the ceiling. He sits down on the camp bed, facing the corridor of death, and takes his face in his hands. For a fraction of a second, the urge to go and see how the prisoner is doing torments him, but he bears it and remains seated where he is. His heart is beating hard enough to break. Sweat covers his face, runs down his back; he doesn't move. In his mind, he hears Musarrat's voice. *You're living through the only moments that make life worthwhile. . . . In love, even beasts become divine. . . .* Atiq curls himself around his sorrow, trying to contain it. The tremor in his shoulders quickly starts again, and a long groan forces him to his knees. He prostrates himself, with his forehead in the dust, and begins reciting every prayer he can think of. . . .

"Atiq."

He starts awake, facedown on the floor. He has fallen asleep while praying. Behind him, the window reveals the first glimmers of the dawn.

A woman in a burqa is standing before him.

"What is it? Are the militiawomen here already?"

The woman looking at him through the latticed eyeholes in her hood pulls it back.

It's Musarrat.

Atiq leaps to his feet and looks around. "How did you get in?"

"I found the door open."

"My God, what was I thinking?" he says. Then, after a brief pause to recover his wits, he asks, "What are you doing here? What do you want?"

"A miracle happened tonight," she says. "My prayers and your prayers joined together, and the Lord heard them. I think your wishes are going to be granted."

"What are you talking about? What miracle?"

"I saw tears fall from your eyes. I thought, If what I see is true, then nothing is completely lost. You, crying? Even when I was pulling the shrapnel out of your flesh, I never managed to get a single whimper out of you. Eventually, I got used to the idea that your heart was fossilized. For a long time, I've believed that nothing could ever really touch you to your soul or fill you with dreams. I've watched you becoming the shadow of yourself day after day, as insensible to your disappointments as rocks are to erosion, even though it's destroying them. War is a monstrosity, and its children take after it. Because that's the way things are, I agreed to share my life with someone whose only ambition was to court death. At least that gave me a reason to believe that I wasn't responsible for my failure with you. And then last night, I saw with my own eyes the man I thought was beyond redemption put his head in his hands and weep. I said, This proves that there's still some light of humanity burning in him; it hasn't gone out altogether. I've come here to fan that flame until it becomes brighter than the day."

"But what are you talking about?"

"I'm saying that my failure was indeed my own fault. You were unhappy because I wasn't able to give your life a meaning. If your eyes could never make your smiles seem sincere, that was because of me. I never gave you any children, or anything to console you for not having them. Whenever you took me, your arms were reaching for someone they never found. Whenever you looked at me, sad memories came back to you. It was clear to me that I was only a shadow taking your shadow's place, and I was ashamed of myself every time you turned away. I wasn't the woman you had fallen in love with; I was the nurse who took care of you and gave you shelter, the one you married to show your gratitude."

"Your illness has affected your reason, Musarrat. Go back home now."

"I tried to be beautiful and desirable for you. When I saw that I couldn't, I suffered. I'm made of flesh and blood, Atiq; every one of your discontented sighs strikes me like a whip. I'm like a ewe, sniffing around for her lamb when it's wandered a little too far from the flock and the hour is getting late. How many times have I caught myself nuzzling your clothes like that! How many times have I sinned by not recognizing that our lot is God's will! I wondered why this was happening to you, why this was happening to me, but never why it was happening to us."

"What exactly do you want?"

"I want another miracle. When I saw the tears in your eyes, I thought I saw heaven opening up and revealing its most beautiful gift. And I told myself that the woman who could move you so deeply must not die."

"I don't understand you."

"Why try to understand something whose very nature is perplexity? Whatever arrives hastens something else's departure—that's the way of the world. There's nothing wrong with resigning yourself to what you can't prevent; whether we're healthy or sickly isn't up to us. What I'm here to say is simple and terrible, but it's also necessary, and we both have to accept it. What's life, and what's death? They have the same value; they cancel each other out."

When Musarrat approaches him, Atiq retreats. She tries to take his hands; he clasps them behind his back. The dawning sun lights up his wife's face. Musarrat is at peace, and she has never been so beautiful.

"In this country, there are many mistakes but never any regrets. The question of execution or mercy, of death or life, isn't resolved by deliberation. No, such decisions are made according to the whim of the moment. Tell her you pleaded her cause with an influential mullah. Say you were successful—there's no need to go into details. She doesn't ever have to know what happened. In a little while, before they come to get her, lock her in your office. I'll slip into her cell. It won't be anything but one burqa taking another's place. Nobody will bother to check the identity of the person underneath. It'll all go very smoothly; you'll see."

"You're absolutely crazy."

"I'm condemned to death anyway. In a few days, or at the latest in a few weeks, the disease eating away at me will finish me off. I'd rather not prolong my suffering needlessly."

Atiq is horrified. He pushes his wife away, then holds his hands out in front of him and implores her to remain where she is. "What you're saying makes no sense," he declares.

"You know very well that I'm right. I've been inspired by the Lord: That woman is not going to die. She'll be everything I couldn't be for you. You have no idea how happy I am this morning. I'll be more useful dead than alive. And at long last, you're being offered a chance. I beg you not to ruin it. Listen to me, just this once. . . ."

Fifteen

⚝

WITH A GREAT SCREECHING of brakes, Qassim Abdul Jabbar brings his 4 × 4 to a halt in front of the
jailhouse. Right behind him comes a little bus filled
with women and children. Preferring to keep his
distance from the malignant atmosphere surrounding the baleful little prison, the driver of the bus
parks it on the other side of the street. Atiq Shaukat
slips into the corridor and stands with his back
against the wall. He pins his trembling hands behind
his buttocks and keeps his eyes on the floor so as not
to betray the intensity of his emotions. He's frightened and cold. His tangled guts rumble and squeal as
though they're about to burst; shooting pains cramp
his legs and threaten to cripple him. The beating of
his blood resounds dully in his temples, like the
blows of a club reverberating through subterranean
galleries. To stave off an attack of panic, he clenches
his teeth and holds his increasingly agitated breath.

Outside in the street, Qassim announces his arrival in his usual way, loudly clearing his throat. This morning, there's something particularly hideous about his phlegmy hawking. Atiq can hear metallic sounds, then the thud of several pairs of feet hitting the ground. Shadows move through the violent light of early morning. Two militiawomen enter the unhealthy darkness of the jailhouse. Despite the steadily rising temperature outside, the interior of the building is cold and damp. Stepping with military precision, the women pass in front of the jailer without a word and move toward the cell at the end of the corridor. Qassim appears in his turn. His massive shoulders fill the doorway, accentuating the semidarkness. Hands on his hips, he shakes his head left and right, performs a few exaggerated contortions, and approaches the jailer while feigning interest in a crack in the ceiling.

"Raise your head, warrior," he says. "You're going to get a crick in your neck, and then you won't be able to look in the mirror properly anymore."

Atiq nods but keeps his eyes fixed on the floor.

The militiawomen reappear, urging the prisoner ahead of them. The two men step back to let them pass. Qassim, who's watching his friend out of the corner of his eye, coughs into his fist. "It's already over," he says softly.

Shivering from head to toe, Atiq hunches his shoulders a little higher.

"You must come with me," Qassim insists.
"There are a few matters I want to discuss with you."

"I can't."

"What's stopping you?"

The jailer opts for silence. Qassim looks around
and glimpses a silhouette crouched in a corner of
Atiq's cubbyhole. "There's someone in your office."

Atiq feels his chest tighten, cutting off his breathing. "My wife."

"I'll bet she wants to go to the stadium."

"Right, exactly right . . . that's just what she
wants."

"So do my wives and my sisters. In fact, they demanded that I requisition the microbus outside. Ah
well, what can you do? Tell your wife to go in the
bus with them. You come with me, and you can pick
her up at the stadium exit when it's over. I've got a
proposal for you, something very dear to my heart,
and I have to tell you about it."

Thrown into confusion, Atiq casts around for a
way out of his plight, but Qassim's heavy voice pre-
vents him from concentrating: "What's the matter?
Are you trying to avoid me?"

"I'm not trying to avoid you."

"What, then?"

Atiq, caught off guard, slouches toward his office,
half shutting his eyes in an attempt to bring some order into his thoughts. Everything around him ap-

pears to be picking up speed, overtaking him, jostling him about. He's unsure how to cope with this completely unexpected turn of events. And never before has the look in Qassim's eye seemed so penetrating, so alert. It's making Atiq sweat all over. A vertiginous tide rolls over him, scanting his breath and sawing at his hamstrings. He stops in the doorway, reflects for a couple of seconds, then shuts the door behind him. The woman sitting on the camp bed stares at him. He can't distinguish her eyes, but her stiffness makes him even more uneasy than he already is.

"You see?" he mutters. "Our prayers have been answered. You're free. The man waiting outside has just confirmed it. They've dropped all the charges against you. You can go back home today."

"Who were the women I saw passing in the hallway?"

"This is a women's prison. Women often come and go here."

"Did they take away a prisoner?"

"That's no concern of yours. The window of yesterday is shut; let's open the window of tomorrow. You're free. That's what counts."

"So I can go now?"

"Of course. But before you do, I'm going to take you to some other women. They're waiting in a little bus right outside. There's no need to tell them who you are or where you come from. In fact, they mustn't know.... The bus will drop you off at the stadium, where some official ceremonies are under way."

"I want to go home."

"Hush! Don't talk so loud."

"I don't care to go to the stadium."

"You must. It won't take long. When the rally's over, I'll wait for you at the exit and take you to a place where you'll be safe."

In the corridor, Qassim clears his throat as a signal to the jailer that it's time to go.

Zunaira stands up. Atiq walks her to the bus, then returns to the 4 × 4 and gets into the front seat next to Qassim. He doesn't look, not even once, into the back of the vehicle, where the two militiawomen and their prisoner are sitting.

THE MULLAHS' diatribes, broadcast through a battery of loudspeakers, echo amid the surrounding ruins. Intermittently, the stadium vibrates with ovations and hysterical clamoring. The crowd grows steadily, for spectators keep streaming in from all parts of the city. Despite the double and triple cordons formed by the forces of order, the atmosphere around the arena is pregnant with excitement. Qassim first directs the little bus to a less congested gate, ushers the ladies out, and turns them over to some militiawomen, ordering them to seat the women in the reserved stands. Then, satisfied on this point, he climbs back into his 4 × 4 and charges onto the field, where armed Taliban agents are bustling about with excessive enthusiasm. A few bodies dangling from ropes here and there testify that the public executions have already begun. The stands are filled to over-flowing with people packed shoulder to shoulder. Many of them have come in order to avoid harass-ment; they witness the horrors, but they remain pas-sive and make no demonstrations. Others, who have chosen to assemble as close as possible to the platform where the dignitaries of the apocalypse are lounging, do everything in their power to get themselves no-ticed; their inordinate (not to say morbid) jubilation and their discordant shouts repel even the religious authorities.

Atiq leaps to the ground and stations himself in front of the 4 × 4, his eyes fixed on the section of the stadium reserved for women. In each of them, he thinks he recognizes Zunaira. Detached from reality, impregnably barricaded, body and soul, inside his delirium, Atiq hears neither the mullahs' sermons nor the crowd's applause. Nor does he seem to see the thousands of onlookers who fill the stands in bestial packs, their mouths more rank and pestilential than their beards. As Atiq tries to guess the location of the woman he's determined to protect, his burning eyes relegate all the rest of the world to oblivion.

A sudden uproar on one side of the stadium gives

rise to some sinister ululations. Agents of the Taliban police hustle one of the "damned" to his destiny; on the pitch, a man with a knife is waiting for him. This part of the program lasts only long enough for the accomplishment of a few simple movements: The bound prisoner is forced to his knees; the knife glitters before it slits his throat. In the stands, sporadic applause pays tribute to the executioner's dexterity. The bloody corpse is tossed onto a stretcher. Next!

Atiq is concentrating so hard on the rows of burqas ranged like a blue wall above his head that he doesn't see the militiawomen lay hold of their prisoner. They walk her to the middle of the field; then two men escort her to the site reserved for her. A peremptory voice orders her to kneel. She complies, and as she raises her eyes behind the grille of her mask for the last time, she catches sight of Atiq, standing with his back to her over by the 4 × 4. At the moment when she feels the muzzle of the rifle brush against the back of her skull, she prays that the jailer won't turn around. In the next instant, the weapon fires, carrying off in its blasphemy an unfinished prayer.

Atiq doesn't know whether the ceremonies have lasted a few hours or an eternity. The stretcher-bearers finish stacking the corpses onto a trailer pulled by a tractor. A particularly trenchant sermon closes the festivities. Immediately thereafter, thousands of the faithful pour onto the field for the general prayer. A mullah with the air of a sultan leads

the ritual while fanatical police agents harry late-
comers. As soon as the prestigious guests depart, the
crowd begins to ebb and flow in savage waves before
converging on the exits. Incredible melees break out,
so violent that the forces of order are obliged to beat
a retreat. When the burqas start filing out of the
stands, Atiq joins a large gathering of men outside.
Qassim is there, hands on hips, visibly pleased with
his performance. The public executions have gone
off smoothly, without a single hitch, and Qassim's
convinced that his contribution to this success has not
escaped the notice of the holy men at the top. He can
already see himself promoted to the directorship of
the country's biggest prison.

The first women emerge from the stadium, to be
quickly retrieved by their men. The women—some
of them burdened with several children—leave the
area in more or less uniform little groups. As the
crowd disperses, the hubbub dies down and the en-
virons of the stadium grow quiet. The throngs making their way back to the center of the city disappear
inside clouds of dust, cut into sections by the Taliban's trucks, which follow one another in an anar-
chic convoy.

Qassim has recognized his harem in the midst of
the crowd and directed them, with a movement of
his head, to the bus, parked and waiting under a tree.
"If you want," he says to Atiq, "I can drop you off at
home, you and your wife."

"That's not necessary," Atiq says.

"I don't mind—it's only a little out of my way."

"I've got some things to do in town."

"All right, as you wish. I hope you think about what I said."

"Of course I will. . . ."

Qassim waves and hurries away to catch up with his women.

And Atiq keeps waiting for his woman. The crowd of people around him shrinks away to nothing. Soon there's only a little cluster of shaggy individuals still keeping him company, and after a few minutes these disappear in their turn, dragging a number of rustling burqas in their wake. When Atiq comes back to himself, he realizes that there's no longer anyone around. There's only the dust-laden sky, the wide-open stadium gate, and the silence—a wretched silence, as deep as an abyss. Incredulous, completely disoriented, Atiq looks around; he's alone, absolutely alone. Seized by panic, he rushes into the stadium. The pitch, the stands, the special platform—all are deserted. Refusing to admit the truth, he runs to the section reserved for women. The naked stone steps are depressingly empty. He goes back down to the field and starts running back and forth like a maniac. The ground undulates under his feet. The deserted stands start whirling around him, empty, empty, empty. A mounting wave of nausea forces him to stop for a moment, but he immediately returns to his frenzied sprinting. The commotion of his breathing threatens to overwhelm the stadium, the city, the entire country. Bewildered, terrified, with his heart about to leap from his throat, Atiq returns to the middle of the pitch, exactly at the spot where there is a pool of coagulated blood. Taking his head in his hands, he stubbornly examines all the sections of the stadium, one by one. Suddenly, realizing the magnitude of the silence, he sinks to his knees, crying out like a stricken beast. As terrible as the fall of a Titan, his howl echoes across the arena: *Zunaira!*

THE FIRST STREAKS of night have gone methodically to work, putting out the last twilight fires in the ashen sky. The daylight has already retreated, step by step, to the uppermost part of the stands, while insidious tentacular shadows spread their cloaks on the earth to welcome the night. Far off, the sounds of the city are dying down. And in the stadium, where a breeze freighted with ghosts is preparing to blow, the concrete tiers lurk in sepulchral silence. Atiq, who has waited and prayed as never before, finally raises his head. The utter misery of his surroundings calls him to order; he has nothing more to do inside these ghastly walls. Pushing himself off the ground with one hand, he rises to his feet. His legs wobble uncertainly. He tries one step, then two, and manages to make his way to the stadium gate. Outside, night has buried the ruins in darkness. A few beggars emerge from their hole; their voices are sleepy enough to make their lamentations convincing. Farther off, some boys armed with wooden swords and rifles carry on the morning's ceremonies; they have bound some of their comrades in the center of a blasted square and are preparing to execute them. Aging idlers watch the boys with smiles on their faces, diverted and touched by the exactness of the youngsters' re-creation. Atiq goes where his legs take him. He feels as though a cloud drifts under his feet. A single name—Zunaira—insistent but inaudible, fills his parched mouth. He passes his little prison, then Nazeesh's house. Full night finds him at the end of an alleyway littered with rubble. Fleeting silhouettes pierce him through and through. When he reaches his house, his legs betray him again, and he collapses in the patio.

Stretched out on his back, Atiq contemplates the moon. Tonight, it's perfectly round, like a silver apple suspended in the air. When he was little, he would spend long hours contemplating it. Sitting on a mound far from the family shack, he'd try to understand how such a heavy star could float in space, and he'd wonder if creatures like his fellow villagers worked the fields on the moon and pastured their goats there. His father joined him once, and it was then that he explained to Atiq the mystery of the moon. "It's only the sun," he told the boy. "After shining conscientiously all day long, the sun gets carried away and tries to violate the secrets of the night. But what he sees is so unbearable that he blanches and loses all his heat."

For a long time, Atiq believed this story. And even today, he still can't stop believing it. What's so frightful about the night that it makes the sun lose all his color?

Gathering the remnants of his strength, Atiq drags himself inside the house. His fumbling hands knock over the lamp. He makes no light; he knows that the least glimmer would strike him blind. His fingers slide along the wall until they come to the doorway of the room that used to be his wife's. He gropes around for her straw mattress and collapses onto it. Choking with sobs, he seizes the blanket in a desperate embrace: "Musarrat, my poor Musarrat, what have you done to us?"

He lies down on the pallet, draws his knees up against his belly, and makes himself very, very small. . . .

"ATIQ."

He starts awake.

A woman is standing in the center of the room. Her opalescent burqa glitters in the darkness. Dumbfounded, Atiq energetically rubs his eyes. The woman doesn't vanish. She's still in the same place, afloat in a luminous blur.

"I thought you were gone for good," he mumbles, trying to get up. "I thought I'd never see you again."

"You were mistaken."

"Where did you go? I looked for you everywhere."

"I wasn't far away—I was hiding."

"I almost went crazy."

"I'm here now."

Clinging to the wall, Atiq gets to his feet. He's shaking like a leaf. The woman opens her arms. "Come," she says.

He runs to her and presses himself against her, like a child returned to its mother. "Oh, Zunaira, Zunaira, what would've become of me without you?"

"That's not a question anymore."

"I was so afraid."

"That's because it's so dark in here."

"I left the lamps unlit on purpose. And I see no reason to light them now. Your face will shine on me more brightly than a thousand candles. Please, lift your hood and let me dream of you."

She takes a step backward and turns up the top of her burqa. Atiq cries out in fright and recoils. She isn't Zunaira anymore; she's Musarrat, and a rifle shot has blown away half of her face.

Atiq wakes up screaming, thrusting out his hands to push away the horror. Covered with sweat, his eyes bulging, he realizes only after several seconds that he's been having a nightmare.

Outside, the day is dawning, and so are the sorrows of the world.

LOOKING LIKE HIS own ghost, Atiq drifts toward the cemetery. He's wearing no turban and carrying no whip; his trousers hang low on his hips, barely held up by a poorly buckled belt. As he walks, he doesn't so much move forward as haul himself along, with his eyes rolled up and devastation in his every step. His untied shoelaces trace serpentine arabesques in the dirt. His right shoe has burst open, exposing to the sun a misshapen toe with a split nail outlined in blood. He must have slipped and fallen somewhere, as his right side is stained with mud and his elbow is skinned. He looks like a drunk, like a man who doesn't know where he is or where he's going. From time to time, he stops and braces himself against a wall: bent over from the waist, hands on his knees, vacillating between his urge to vomit and his need to catch his breath. His dark face, under its thatch of unkempt beard, is as wrinkled as an overripe quince; his deeply lined forehead and swollen eyes complement his appearance of advanced deterioration; his misery is shrill, unignorable. The rare pedestrians who cross his path look at him with fearful eyes. Some of them make broad detours to avoid him, and the children playing here and there keep him under careful surveillance.

Atiq has no idea of the terror he's arousing. His head is a weight on his shoulders, his movements are erratic, and he's only vaguely aware of the maze of little streets. He hasn't eaten for three days. Fasting and grief have drained him. Saliva like dried milk stains the corners of his mouth, and he keeps blowing his nose into his cupped hand. He needs several heaves to detach himself from the wall and set himself in motion. His legs buckle under his sagging carcass. He's been stopped twice by squads of Taliban police, who suspected him of inebriation; someone even struck him and ordered him to return home at once. Atiq noticed none of this. As soon as he was let go, he continued on his way to the cemetery, as though summoned there by a mysterious call.

A family consisting of women dressed in rags and children whose little faces are streaked with grime is gathered around a fresh grave. Farther off, a mule driver tries to repair one of his carriage wheels, which has struck a large stone and sprung from its axle. A few scrawny dogs with muddy muzzles and cocked ears sniff along the paths. Atiq staggers about amid the mounds, without gravestones and without epitaphs, that blister the arid terrain of the cemetery. The graves are only holes in the ground, haphazardly dug and filled in with dirt and gravel and caked earth. They lie in an alarming jumble that adds a tragic note to the sadness of the place. Atiq lingers over these bare tombs, squatting now and then to touch one of them with his fingertips. Sometimes he steps over the little mounds; sometimes he stumbles on them and mutters. After going in a circle, he realizes that he won't be able to identify Musarrat's last resting place because he hasn't the vaguest idea where to look for it. He spies a gravedigger eating a piece of dried meat, goes over to him, and asks him where the woman who was executed at the municipal stadium yesterday is buried. The gravedigger shows him a pile of dirt a stone's throw away and returns with hearty appetite to his meal.

Atiq collapses before his wife's grave, takes his head in his hands, and stays that way until late in the afternoon—without a word, without a groan, without a prayer. His curiosity piqued, the gravedigger comes over to check whether the strange visitor is awake. He tells Atiq that the sun is dangerously hot, that he'll be sorry if he doesn't get out of it. Atiq fails to grasp what he's doing wrong. He continues to stare undeterred at Musarrat's grave. Then, when his head is crackling and his eyes are half blind, he rises and leaves the cemetery without looking back. Leaning sometimes on a wall, sometimes on a tree, he wanders through a series of alleyways until the sight of a woman stepping out of a house with a mansard roof seems almost to clear his head. She's wearing a faded burqa with holes in its skirts, and down-at-the-heel shoes. Atiq stations himself in the middle of the narrow street and waits to intercept her. The woman veers off to one side; Atiq catches her by the arm and tries to hold her back. With a jerk, she frees herself from his clutches and runs away. *Zunaira*, he says to her, *Zunaira*. The woman comes to a stop at the end of the alley, stares at him curiously, and disappears. Atiq runs after her, holding out one arm as though trying to spear a smoke ring. In another narrow lane, he bears down upon another woman, who is sitting on the threshold of a ruined house. When she sees him coming, she goes back inside and closes the door behind her. Atiq turns around and sees a yellow burqa slipping toward the district square. He follows it, still holding one arm out in front of him. *Zunaira, Zunaira* . . . Children hurry out of his path, frightened by this disheveled man with bulging pupils and bluish lips who seems to be stalking his own insanity. The yellow burqa stops in front of one of the houses; Atiq rushes toward it, reaching it at the moment when the door opens. *Where did you go? I waited for you at the stadium exit, just as we agreed, and you didn't come out to me. . . .*

The yellow burqa tries to free itself from his painful grasp. *You're mad! Let me go or I'll scream. . . .*

I won't leave you alone anymore, Zunaira. Since you can't find me, you'll never have to look for me again.

I'm not your Zunaira, you poor fool. If you don't get out of here, my brothers will kill you.

Lift your hood. I want to see your face, your beautiful houri's face. . . .

The burqa sacrifices its side panel to his grasp and vanishes. Some boys who have assisted at this scene pick up stones and begin flinging them at the madman until he retreats the way he came. One of the projectiles has split the side of Atiq's head open, and blood is pouring over his ear as he starts running, at first with little steps, but then, as he approaches the square, with longer and longer strides, his breathing hoarse, his nostrils dripping, foam boiling out of his mouth. *Zunaira, Zunaira*, he babbles, tossing aside bystanders in his search for a burqa. As his frenzy mounts, he starts chasing women down and—O sacrilege!—lifting their veils above their heads. *Zunaira, I know you're in there. Come out of your hiding place. There's nothing to fear. No one will hurt you. I've taken care of everything. I won't let anyone bother you. . . .*

Indignant cries ring out. Atiq doesn't hear them. His hands snatch at veils, violently tearing them away, sometimes capsizing the cornered women. Whenever one of them resists, he throws her to the ground and hauls her around in the dust, only releasing her when he's certain that she's not the one he's searching for. The first cudgel blow lands on the back of his neck, but he does not falter. As though catapulted by a supernatural force, he continues his wild career. Soon the scandalized crowd fans out to contain him. The women scatter, screaming; he manages to seize a few, tears their clothes, lifts their heads by the hair. The cudgel is followed by whips, and these by fists and feet. The men who have been "dishonored" trample their women to get at the madman. *Demon! Fiend!* Atiq has a vague sensation of being carried away by a landslide. He's kicked by a thousand shabby shoes, buffeted by a thousand sticks, lashed by a thousand whips. *Pervert! Monster!* Crushed under the tumult, he collapses. The furious pack, sensing the kill, hurls itself upon him. He has just enough time to notice that his shirt has disappeared, torn to shreds by vicious fingers, that blood is running down his chest and arms in thick streams, and that his eyebrows have burst, rendering it impossible for him to measure the unquenchable fury of his assailants. A few fragmented shouts reach his ears amid the rain of blows that keep him pinned to the ground. *Hang him! Crucify him! Burn him alive!* All of a sudden, his head starts to oscillate, and his surroundings slide into darkness. There follows a solemn, intense silence, and as he closes his eyes, Atiq entreats his ancestors that his sleep may be as unfathomable as the secrets of the night.